Suddenly the wave of emotion was more than he could handle. His chest became so tight that he found it difficult to breathe. There was an aching pressure behind his eyes. He knew it was his natural impulse to hold back his tears no matter how hard he had to strain. He took a deep breath and then another. He wanted nothing more than to stop reliving that night. He wished he could scrape it from his memory permanently. But he knew Gaia needed to hear it. And he also knew he needed to say it.

"I tried to protect you, Gaia. . . ."

And then he was crying. He despised crying. He'd always thought it was weak and useless, self-indulgent. He hadn't even let himself cry that night. Instead he'd gone numb, blank, shut down.

Of course, that was exactly why he couldn't let it happen again.

Don't miss any books in this thrilling series:

FEARLESS™

Available from POCKET PULSE

FEARLESS™

MISSING

FRANCINE PASCAL

POCKET PULSE

New York London Toronto Sydney Singapore

To Jonathan Rubin

An *Original* Publication *of* POCKET BOOKS

POCKET PULSE, published by
Pocket Books, a division of Simon & Schuster, Inc.
1230 Avenue of the Americas, New York, NY 10020

Produced by 17th Street Productions,
an Alloy Online, Inc. company
33 West 17th Street
New York, NY 10011

ISBN: 0-7434-1248-6

First Pocket Pulse Paperback printing March 2001

10 9 8 7 6 5 4 3 2 1

Fearless™ is a trademark of Francine Pascal.
POCKET PULSE and colophon are
trademarks of Simon & Schuster, Inc.

Printed in the U.S.A.

MISSING

She couldn't
even begin
to accept
what was
happening,
but it
didn't
matter. Her
brain had
shut down.

**pure
rage**

IT WAS ALL HAPPENING SO FAST.

One moment melted quickly and imperceptibly into the next. Gaia found herself unable to remember the events of the last three minutes, let alone the last three hours—when she was still in Manhattan, mired in

Totally Novel Idea

that fluorescent den of Urban Outfitter dimwits called The Village School. How had she gotten to this moment?

Her breaths were quick and shallow, her heart racing. Her stomach seemed to be dancing at the top of her throat. She gripped the chrome armrests of her airline seat tightly—so tightly that her hands were going numb.

This could very possibly be a dream, she thought.

Somewhere in the last three hours, Gaia Moore had begun a new life.

The 747 jumbo jet made a slow, sweeping turn on the runway. Gaia actually considered pinching herself—but ruled it out as being too much of a cliché. No, if she was going to pinch someone for a reality check, it would be the man sitting next to her in the window seat . . . decked out in his thick black overcoat, Armani suit, and slicked-back hair. He was like a vision from some film noir. He was too good to be true.

Uncle Oliver, she thought, savoring each syllable. Looking at him—her blood relative, her family—she tried once again to accept the notion of good fortune, of things going right for a change. Thinking this way wasn't her strong suit. Humongous waves of optimism were totally alien to her. All this newfound love in her life was almost making her queasy. Like an overload of Krispy Kreme doughnuts. She was on a sugar high—but a *pleasant* one. A wonderful one.

The only possible crimp in her euphoria was the fact that she was leaving Sam Moon behind. But that was only temporary. Yes, there was a sort of twisted irony involved in loving someone for so long from afar—and being separated literally at the moment of connection . . . but he would wait for her.

Wouldn't he?

Of course he would. He had to wait.

Anyway, what mattered most—*all* that mattered, really—was that her uncle had kept his promise: a promise he'd made to her the first night he ever spoke to her, the night those sick thugs had almost killed Sam Moon and then almost killed her. Had he been even a moment later, Gaia's throat would have been slit from ear to ear. But he had appeared out of nowhere—a white knight out of the shadows of Washington Square Park—and he'd taken down that knife-wielding bastard with one perfect shot.

Gaia was barely conscious by then, but she could still hear her uncle's words. Kneeling close to her, keeping her safe, he'd made his solemn promise: "I'll come back for you," he said. "I swear it."

And here he was, right beside her.

That a family member would keep a promise to Gaia was a totally novel idea. But it was one she could see herself getting used to. And she was ready to repay the favor. She knew Uncle Oliver was very sick— stricken with a resurgence of cancer that was now attacking his pancreas. But there were doctors in Germany who could help him. And Gaia believed in her heart that even if his indomitable strength and those specialists' treatments weren't enough to cure him, love and gratitude would do the trick.

Because if there's one thing Gaia had learned in the five years that her body and soul had taken a beating (and one thing that she *never* would have admitted under even the most severe torture), it was this: No one—no person or animal or creature of any kind— could truly live without some kind of family. One could survive, yes. Gaia had proved that time and time again. But truly living was impossible.

And that's just what Gaia was going to make damn sure her uncle did.

Live.

The engines of the 747 began to rumble, whirring at an increasing pitch as the plane cruised down the runway. Gaia watched as the yellow markers on the ground passed by the oval window one by one, blurring into a solid strip of neon lightning. Adrenaline poured through her veins. She felt the jet's wheels spinning beneath her, poised to float off the ground at any second.

Without even thinking, Gaia reached for Oliver's hand, clasping her fingers with his. He turned to her. A warm smile spread across his rugged, shaded face, the familial connection seeming almost electric, as if their common blood were joining at the fingertips.

And then she realized that she'd spent so much time listening to her own thoughts, she hadn't even said a word to her uncle since they'd boarded the plane.

"I can't believe this," she murmured. "I can't believe we're really—"

"Shhh." Her uncle squeezed her hand firmly, raising his index finger to his lips to silence her. He raised his head slightly over his seat and scanned the front and back of the passenger area. Gaia couldn't help but notice the tension in his grip, the unsettled look in his eye. And she remembered one very important fact— something she'd managed to forget in all her disorienting excitement: She and Uncle Oliver were on the lam. Technically Gaia was still a minor and still under the care of the Niven family—so legally speaking, she was actually being *kidnapped*. It was almost funny. Oliver was obviously surveying the plane to make sure that nobody had followed them. . . .

The Niven family.

Yeah. Some family. She shifted in her seat. Harsh

memories began to stomp all over her familial buzz, like giant footsteps—trampling down on her just as the nose of the plane lifted into the white winter sky. There was George Niven, the hapless absentee parent . . .

And then there was Ella.

Ella. Once known simply as her "stepmonster." The woman who'd hated Gaia so much, she'd actually put a professional hit out on her. Gaia couldn't think of her former foster mother without a bewildering rush of emotion. The events were still too recent, too painful. First Ella was an airheaded bitch. Then she was a murderous spy. And then she was just a very sad figure who'd traded her own life for Gaia's. Somehow, in the last hours of Ella's wasted life, all of Gaia's feelings for her had shifted. She'd realized that Ella was really a victim much like herself. . . .

Another tragic victim of Gaia's father.

In the end, though, Ella was the one person who'd actually had the guts and decency to tell Gaia the truth about the man—that he was a dark-hearted sadist who'd named himself for the satanic Norse god of the underworld: *Loki.* Nausea tore through Gaia's stomach. Loki had made Ella's life a living hell right up until her death. But that was a far cry from his worst crime. Yes . . . because Loki was also the man that had killed Gaia's mother.

My father killed my mother.

The sentence echoed through Gaia's head again. She had

6

done everything in her power to keep that horrific mantra out of her mind, but it was impossible. Whenever she let it in for a moment, it would haunt her for hours at a time—

My father killed my mother.

She shook her head. Today that thought was forbidden. Her father faded farther into the distance with every second the plane climbed higher in the air. Her uncle had saved her—from her father and from everything else.

As the plane broke past the thick layer of clouds that made New York City seem so dank and lifeless, a burst of golden sunlight and royal blue sky invaded Gaia's eyes. She had to smile. It was literally as if she were entering . . . well, heaven. The only thing missing from the moment was some chorus of angelic sopranos singing in unison. The past was officially behind her. She'd left it in the clouds. Uncle Oliver seemed to know it, too. The tension seemed to drop from his body, his entire posture relaxing as he sank comfortably into his chair and unbuttoned his jacket.

"We made it," Gaia whispered, squeezing her uncle's arm. "Now we can chill."

"I'm sorry," he murmured. "I just wanted to get you safely on the plane and into the air."

"I know, Uncle Oli—"

"No," he interrupted, pulling off his sunglasses. "Gaia . . . look at me. I didn't want to confuse you."

Gaia looked into his eyes. Her heart seemed to freeze. Something wasn't right. . . .

"I'm not Oliver," he said gently.

Time thundered to a standstill.

He cupped his hand on her cheek, caressing her face lightly with his thumb.

"Gaia, it's me," he said smiling, his translucent blue eyes clouding with tears. His voice began to crack. "It's . . . *me*."

Horror prevented her from reacting. It was as if a cold steel rod had just been shoved down her spine, sending a ripple of pain through every limb. She could feel her face filling with blood, turning bright red, overheating—

Loki.

The man who killed her mother was touching her face. Electricity simmered in her veins. There was no fear, of course. Only rage. Pure rage.

"Look at me," her father whispered gently.

Reflex took over. Gaia snapped her elbow into her father's face with the force of a sling blade, whipping back his head and bashing it into the airplane window. The blow instantly knocked him cold. She couldn't even begin to accept what was happening, but it didn't matter. Her brain had shut down. All she had now were strategic reflexes from years of combat training—ironically, training provided by the bastard she'd just pummeled. Her only impulses were to punish her enemy and protect herself. He'd taught her well. She leaped from her seat and ran for the bathroom at the back of the plane, slamming the flimsy door behind her and locking it.

Some idiot stewardess started pounding on the door.

"Young lady," she whined in a deep southern drawl, knocking away. "Please take your seat until the captain—"

Gaia's fury exploded from her, beyond her control—like that of a caged tiger. "Stay away from me!" she shrieked. She caught a glimpse of herself in the bathroom mirror and realized that tears were streaming down her face. She channeled her emotion into her hands as she ripped up everything in sight, toilet paper, seat covers, paper towels; she punched a huge dent into the chrome towel holder.

And then just as quickly, all the energy drained from her body.

She slid down to the floor, cramped in the small space between the sink and the toilet, her legs pushed up against the wall of the bathroom, her back leaning against the door.

She was trapped. She'd been duped.

What a huge steaming load of *bullshit*.

"Why?" she heard herself asking as she lifted her head and pounded it back against the door. She wasn't talking to anyone in particular—not her father or her uncle Oliver. She was just shouting at Fate.

"Why are you doing this to me? Why can't you *help* me for once?"

Top Five Reasons I Should Kill
My Father Right Now

1. It would be a good way to pass
   some time on the flight. (I
   saw the list of movies, and
   they all suck.)
2. The human race would be much
   better off without him.
3. In all likelihood, I would be
   taken back to New York and
   thrown in prison for the rest
   of my life—where I could
   really have some time to
   think and catch up on some
   reading and work out and make
   lifelong friends. Or maybe
   I'd be executed, in which
   case my miserable life would
   come to an end.
4. Killing my father would free
   up his in-flight dinner; I
   could get two desserts.
5. I would never mistake him for
   my uncle again.

Floating in
this wacked-
out state,
bathed in
icy sweat, **caged**
he could
have sworn **tiger**
he'd heard
Gaia Moore
call to him.

"GAIA . . ."

Ed Fargo awoke to a shock of convulsions. He was only semiconscious. His arms and torso were shivering. He must have been buried up to his neck in ice cubes. Either that or thrashing from a blast of high-voltage electroshock treatment. Floating in this wacked-out state, bathed in icy sweat, he could have sworn he'd heard Gaia Moore call to him. But then he began to realize that wherever he was, Gaia was definitely *not* there with him. Nope. Ed was miles away from anyone or anyplace he knew.

Croaking Like Some Mafia Guy

And wherever it was, it was *white.* Very, very white.

"The shivering's quite normal, Ed," a familiar voice assured him in a kind but deliberate tone. "You'll be warm in no time. Pam, let's get Ed another blanket."

"Of course, Doctor," a voice replied.

Dr. Feldman, Ed thought. His brain was beginning to function again. *Yeah. I'm in the hospital. . . .*

And then it hit him. He remembered the mask being placed over his nose and mouth and the needle piercing the vein of his arm, pumping him full of anesthesia. He remembered being asked to count backward from a hundred, but he didn't even remember ninety-eight. Now, what seemed like only seconds later . . . he was here. So this could only be the recovery room. His surgery was done.

Ed's eyes began to make sense of his surroundings as they finally adjusted to the stark glare of the fluorescent lights. Bleached white lab coats surrounded Ed's bed in a claustrophobic huddle, topped by a bizarre collection of pasty faces. He sort of remembered the face of one of the doctors—Ramirez was his name, he thought. But the rest of them were just one big freak show.

Each doctor was scribbling his or her own notes . . . but no one was talking. Ed searched their faces anxiously.

Hello? People? Somebody say something. I'm freaking out here—

Well. Their silence told Ed everything he needed to know. If no one was talking, that could only mean one thing. The surgery had to have been a failure. No one wanted to tell him that they'd gotten his hopes up for nothing. It was so ridiculous. Ed hadn't gotten his hopes up in the first place. *They* had. It had taken God knows how long, but Ed had come to accept the fact that he'd never walk again. He'd finally stopped fantasizing about running up a flight of stairs or stepping between two people on a crowded street *unnoticed*. He'd even overcome his yearning to be back on his board—to be "Shred"

13

again, floating on his skateboard down a ten-foot rail. . . .

Dr. Feldman had tried to do this psych job on him. He'd offered up this new cutting-edge laser surgery, dangling the promise of working legs right in his face—and for what? To inject a nice fresh batch of disappointment into his life? Dr. Feldman had him right back where he started two years ago, with that same sickening stupid question he'd never wanted to ask again.

Will I walk or not?

Almost as if by instinct, Ed struggled forward in his bed and made a grab for his legs, desperate to see if they'd respond to an instruction from his brain to move. But the movement was met with a flash of pain. It shot through his body like a double-edged blade, snapping his torso back down on the bed.

Shit.

"Whoa, there!" Dr. Feldman warned with a laugh, placing his hand gently on Ed's chest to hold him down. "One day at a time, Tiger."

"Sorry," Ed croaked, wincing and hoarse from postsurgical dry mouth.

The nurse stepped in front of Dr. Feldman and placed another blanket over Ed. He clenched his teeth, trying to ride out the wave of pain. What fun.

"Well, the operation was a success," Dr. Feldman announced matter-of-factly. He made some notes on Ed's chart.

A ... what?

Ed's pain disappeared. Instantly. His eyes bulged. His vision was still blurry, but Dr. Feldman's uncommonly round head suddenly seemed like the most beautiful thing Ed had ever seen.

"It—it," Ed stammered ecstatically, still croaking like some mafia guy in a grade-B mob movie. "It worked? You mean—"

"It doesn't necessarily mean anything," Dr. Feldman interrupted in a more serious tone, swatting Ed's hopes right back at him. He came crashing back down to earth, back into his hospital bed—back into his wheelchair for life. The forgotten pain returned at twice the strength.

"I—I don't . . . ," Ed stammered again. "I don't understand."

Dr. Feldman grabbed the chair at the side of the bed and pulled it up next to Ed, taking a seat so that they were eye to eye. He placed Ed's chart on the bedside table. The pasty-faced crew took a half step away in unison.

"Here's the story," Dr. Feldman said, clearly trying to keep things positive. "Your brain and your legs are connected again . . . they're just not on speaking terms. They need to get to know each other again, and they may not want to at this point. Does that make sense?"

Ed scowled. What was this, *Sesame Street*? He really didn't see the point of metaphor right now.

"Also," the doctor continued, "your leg muscles have completely atrophied. And they may not want to come back."

"So what are you saying?" Ed asked, desperate to drop the double-talk. "Just tell me what I have to do."

"That's the right question, Ed," Dr. Feldman replied. He sighed and looked Ed in the eye. "You're going to have to start physical therapy. It's going to involve a lot of pain and hard work—every day, for hours a day. Frankly, it will be grueling. But it's the only way we're going to get the strength back into those muscles."

Ed nodded as emphatically as he could. He didn't care how hard he had to work. He didn't care how much it hurt. He was ready. "What else?" he asked.

Doctor Feldman offered a little half smile. "You have to have faith," he stated.

"A lot of it."

"OH, I THINK HE'S COMING TO," a disembodied voice announced.

Tom Moore's eyes fluttered open. He found himself staring at a host of concerned faces, hanging over the **Wallop** backs of their airline seats and hunched over him in the aisle. A stewardess caked in makeup thrust an icc pack toward his head.

"I thought you might need this," she cooed in a southern accent. "That's quite a boo-boo you've got there! Is your daughter a ninja or somethin'? You need peanuts and a diet Coke."

"No. Thank you," Tom managed to answer, as politely as he could. His head throbbed. He took the ice pack and raised his fingers to test out the swelling on his bruised cheekbone. The stinging was acute. "My goodness," he said with a sudden smile.

The other passengers cocked their heads, gaping at him. Tom knew they must have all been a little thrown by his reaction to his injury. He hadn't smiled like this in a while—the unfettered smile of a proud father. What a wallop. Gaia's strength was undiminished. In all his days as an operative, thinking back through the countless covert missions he'd been assigned—even when he'd been forced to do battle with the most rigorously trained assassins—he couldn't remember being taken out with such a perfectly aimed, swift, and merciless blow.

But as soon as the smile appeared, it dropped from Tom's face.

She hated him. And he knew why. He'd abandoned her. In her mind, he'd betrayed her—in the worst possible way. Guilt swept through him, overpowering the physical pain, blotting it out. She still didn't know the truth....

"I tell you, the kids to*day*," a woman with a Long Island accent shouted. Tom wasn't altogether sure why she was shouting. She was resting her arms on the seat back right in front of his, staring down at him, peanut crumbs falling from her lips. "*Juvenile delinquents.* Every one of 'em. I have a troubled teen of my *own* at *home* . . . well, not really at home, in *jail.* If they're not out drinkin' their twelve packs of beer and having unprotected sex, then they're out dropping their ecstasy at their rave parties and selling the *loco weed* to a bunch of fourth graders—"

"I don't think you understand," Tom found himself interrupting.

The woman frowned.

He tore off his seat belt and stood, dropping the ice pack to the floor. He glanced around at the other passengers. They were all staring at him. He felt out of control, and it was an emotion he was ill equipped to handle. His life depended on control.

He turned to the stewardess with solemn determination. "Where's my daughter?"

She blinked, then pointed toward the bathrooms at the back of the plane.

Tom walked down the aisle to the locked bathroom and swung the curtain closed that divided the lavatories from the rest of the plane. It was the closest thing to privacy they'd have. He knocked gently on the door.

"Gaia? Are you all right?"

"Stay away," came the harsh reply.

Tom winced. There was such hatred, oozing from each word. "Gaia, please. I—"

"Get away from the door, *Loki!*" she screamed. "*I know who you are.* You . . . you killed her. You killed her! How *could* you?"

Tom staggered away from the door. It was as if a broadsword had been plunged through his chest. Even in the worst of his nightmares, he'd never imagined hearing his daughter speak those words. He knew very well which "her" Gaia meant.

Katia. His sweet Katia. Gaia's mother . . .

"Dear God," he uttered involuntarily.

He's poisoned her mind. Oliver has poisoned her mind.

I've always had a special
place in my heart for rodents. I
was obsessed with hamsters and
gerbils when I was a kid. I was
in love with my pet field mouse
Jonathan.

I think everyone figured I'd
grow out of it. But it hasn't
happened yet.

The fact of the matter is, sitting there curled up in a pathetic
little ball in that heinous,
industrially perfumed airplane
bathroom, I realized just how
close I felt to all those poor
hamsters and gerbils I'd merci-
lessly forced into pethood.
Because when you boil it down to
its essential elements . . . our
lives are really exactly the same.
Meaning mine and the average
rodent's. We both live in the same
ignorant hell.

See, that poor little furry
bastard thinks he's free. He figures, *Hey. I've got free will. I
can go wherever the hell I want.
I can be whatever I want to be.*

G A I A

*I'm just gonna climb right into
this little metal wheel here and
head for the hills.*

Twenty minutes later that
ignorant ball of fluff is sweat-
ing his ass off, panting like an
Alaskan husky on a New York sum-
mer day. He figures he must be at
least a mile farther in his life,
maybe even two. Then he takes a
look around and he sees the
truth. He's right there in the
exact same little piece of shit
wheel, in the exact same little
piece of shit box.

Free will? What a freaking
joke. Sure, he's got the will.
It's the *free* part that's the
problem—see, because he's in a
goddamn *box*. A big glass box. And
sure, he can see the rest of the
world. He can *imagine* being a
part of the rest of the world.
But a few steps forward and—
clank—reality smacks him in his
innocent little black-eyed face.

That's me.

I'm that hamster running my

ass off in Loki's little metal
wheel, in Loki's little glass
box.

How could I have been so
blind? How did I not notice
something when that demented
sicko picked me up at the
airport? How did it all slip
right over my head?

I know the answer.

It's obvious. The only way I'd
miss something like that . . . is
if I wanted to.

I thought *I* had free will. I
thought I'd broken free from my
doom-saturated glue trap of a
life and that I was going to
change it. I thought I could
change my life. What the hell was
I thinking? I was never free from
anything. I was never escaping
anything. The whole time I was
just being suckered into Loki's
plans. He'd been controlling
every move I made.

And my life will always be the
exact same. Nothing will ever
change. My fate was decided long

before I had anything to say
about it. All I'm doing is scampering my little feet in my little wheel, mile after mile. And
to tell you the truth . . . I'm
tired. I'm exhausted.

Romeo (of William Shakespeare
fame) was fortune's fool.

I'm fortune's hamster.

Fortune's sucker. Fortune's
shit-for-brains.

I'll just be scampering my
little feet forever until it's
time for someone to flush me down
this airplane toilet, with its
beautiful crystal blue water and
its reek of human feces and sweet
perfume.

That's who I am.

Oh, well. At least I'm me
again.

I can't even begin to describe
what it feels like to be free and
clear.

There was a moment there about
a month ago when I seriously
thought I'd never be free again.
I felt like every day would just
be another day in hell. Gaia
despised me. Her insane foster
mom had lured me into bed one
night when I was plastered, and
I'd been paying for it every second since. Of course I had no
idea at the time that she was any
relation to Gaia. She just picked
me up at a bar, and I was too
drunk to say no.

Had I known Ella was a fatal
attraction psycho who was going
to kill my roommate, I probably
would have made some adjustments
to the beer goggles.

Ella haunted me every single
day, bombarding me with phone
calls, e-mails, surprise visits.
But once I'd realized just how
sick she was—once she'd forcibly
injected an overdose of heroin

into my roommate Mike Suarez's arm just to threaten me . . . I knew it was probably only a matter of time before she went ahead and killed me.

I'd been walking the city streets for weeks, looking just like those vacant-eyed homeless junkies in Alphabet City. White as a sheet. Dark crimson circles under my eyes. The works. I couldn't sleep. I couldn't think. I couldn't do an ounce of work. My 3.85 average was taking a nosedive.

I was running from Ella. I was desperately searching for Gaia, trying to figure out how to tell her the truth, praying she could find it in her heart to forgive me. I felt like one of those lab rats we use for our tests in class, sitting in a cage while they just dosed me with electric shocks over and over—with nowhere to run.

No, you know what I really felt like?

I felt like Odysseus.

That ultimate of all kick-ass seafaring warriors from Homer's *Odyssey*.

I mean, Odysseus couldn't catch a break. He was out there in his creaky wooden ship, and everyone and everything was trying to take him down. He had to take on the Cyclops, gigantic multiheaded snake beasts; even the *gods* wanted out of the picture. And the whole time all he really wanted was just to get home to his ultrafine wife, eat a good meal, et cetera.

And that was really all I wanted. All these tortured weeks Ella was stalking me, with Mike dying in a hospital bed and my college career going down the toilet, all I'd really wanted the whole time—since the first day I'd seen her—was Gaia. Just to be with her in a quiet moment, and touch her skin, and tell her that I loved her.

And now . . .

I have her. My proverbial ship has come in.

And the worst is over.

Finally. Ella is gone. Mike is gone too, unfortunately, and that still makes me ill. But what I need right now is just some time to breathe like a regular NYU sophomore.

I am due for a nice long stint of normalcy. That's all I want. Just to play chess, write letters to Gaia in Germany until she comes home, and do some serious studying. I mean, I've been dreaming about the day when the biggest thing I had to worry about was an organic chemistry midterm. And that day is today.

I'm free at last. I can think again. I can eat again. I can sleep again.

It was
like being
trapped
in a box
with a
thousand
killer
bees.

KNOCK KNOCK KNOCK.

Detective Shtick

There was an annoying pounding on Sam's dorm-room door.

Knock knock knock.

"Mr. Moon?" an obnoxious voice shouted. "Hey, Mr. Moon, open up, please. Rise and shine."

Sam shook his head and squinted at his bedside clock: 3:43. He didn't have classes for the rest of the day. He'd just wanted to catch a few z's before going to the lab that night . . . and who the hell *was* that? He ripped his sheet off with a loud dissatisfied grunt, straightening out his boxers and running his hands through his unruly curls. He snatched a T-shirt off the floor and tried to pull it over his head with one hand as he went to the door.

"Who is it?" He groaned.

"It's the NYPD."

Suddenly Sam was wide awake. His heart took a brief pause from beating as his neck went stiff and cold. This didn't make any sense. He'd already given his statement to the police. What were they doing back at his dorm? His hands began to shake as he fumbled with the lock on the door—the lock he'd just recently installed for protection against Ella. He cracked open the door. His insides squeezed.

The same two detectives who had interviewed him

before about Mike's murder were shoving their badges in his face yet again. As far as Sam could tell, they'd seemed to have learned their entire detective shtick watching too many episodes of *Law & Order* and *NYPD Blue*.

"Hello, Mr. Moon," the heavyset one stated in an overly formal voice. His thinning hair seemed to be glued on his scalp with some industrial chemical compound. "You may remember us. I'm Detective Bernard. This is my partner, Detective Reilly. You think we might ask you a few more questions about the night of Mike Suarez's murder?"

Sam swallowed. This was not good. The more the cops asked, the greater the chance of uncovering something about Ella—about *him* and Ella.

"I thought I'd answered all your questions," Sam said, trying to keep his lips moving normally as he spoke through the partially opened door. His mouth was dry. "I really told you everything I know. I mean . . . if I knew something else, I'd tell you."

"Oh, we understand, son," Detective Reilly said. Sam could detect the sourest reek of morning-after booze on Reilly's breath. He had the feeling Reilly's pores were always working overtime to excrete the excess Budweiser from his system. "We were just wondering if you'd remembered anything else from that night."

"*No,*" Sam stated. "I just said . . . if I remembered something else, I'd tell you—"

"Hey, did you ever find the movie ticket from that night?" Reilly asked with a feigned you're-my-pal grin.

That movie ticket. Sam didn't think of himself as stupid, but when the cops had asked him where he was that night, he'd been so anxious to keep himself out of it that he'd offered up this moronic lie about a foreign film at the Angelika.

"Nope," Sam answered with his own moronic grin and a shrug. "I checked all my pants, but you know, laundry and whatnot. . . ."

There was a long, awkward pause. Sam could feel beads of sweat running down the back of his neck.

"So you don't remember anything?" Bernard asked again.

Were they deaf? Sam couldn't believe he was still having this inane conversation.

"Do you remember who else was in the dorm that night?" Bernard added quickly.

"Do you remember if anyone was smoking marijuana?" Reilly threw in. "Or using drugs of any kind?"

Sam cringed. "No, Detective," he forced himself to reply. "Don't recall any drugs." He was losing his patience, and his nerves were getting the better of him. His left hand was beginning to inch his door closed in spite of himself. "I'm sorry. But thank you . . . and . . . if I remember something, I'll call you first thing."

"But you don't—," Bernard started.

"I'm sorry," Sam interrupted, slamming the door.

He'd had all he could take. He couldn't believe they were still hounding him. His life was supposed to be smooth sailing from now on—and this was what he had to deal with? He couldn't understand why they couldn't leave it alone. Mike was dead, and Ella was dead. *There was nobody left to blame.* As far as the law went, he was in the clear.

The best thing to do was just to sleep it off. So they had a few more questions. He'd told them he didn't remember anything more. That was that. A few more hours of sleep and things would be back to normal. Maybe he'd even have another dream about Gaia.

Sam pulled off his T-shirt and walked back toward the bed. But somehow he didn't feel sleepy anymore.

"GAIA, PLEASE," HER FATHER'S VOICE

begged through the bathroom door. "You have to listen to me. Oliver has told you so many lies. He's poisoned your mind, sweetheart; please listen—"

"Shut up!" Gaia screamed. Her ears couldn't stand to hear that voice.

Swiss Cheese

It was a voice she'd yearned to hear for so long . . . but it was too upsetting, too disconcerting, too confusing.

That kind voice belonged to a cold, calculating murderer.

"Gaia—"

"Shut up! Shut up! Shut up!" Different scenarios began racing through her head: *Option 1: Subdue him until I can hand him over to the German authorities. Option 2: Just kill him now—avenge my mother's death. Option 3: Just kill myself now—put an end to the tragedy that is clearly my life. . . .*

But she was kidding herself. She had no options. All she could do was sit in that bathroom and rot. It was like being trapped in a box with a thousand killer bees. Nowhere to run. Nothing to do but sit there and get stung over and over by her father's words.

"Don't you understand?" his voice pleaded through the door. "Oliver tricked you, Gaia. I'm not Loki. Oliver is Loki. Somewhere along the way his mind turned. He became mentally ill. His soul just . . . disappeared. He's evil, Gaia. Pure evil—"

"You're lying!" Gaia snapped.

Her body was shaking with anger. Her mind felt like a chunk of Swiss cheese; it was full of gaping holes. Everyone had a different story. Everyone in her life was telling lies. Ella lied for a living. George lied for a living. Her father lied for a living. Oliver wouldn't even tell her what he did for a living, but he sure seemed to be good with a gun, based on the night he'd saved her life. How was she possibly supposed to know whom to believe? The only thing she knew for sure was that Oliver was the only one out of all these people who'd been nothing but nice to her since she met him.

"Oliver saved my life," she shouted harshly. "Is that evil? Saving someone's life? He was there for me when nobody else was. Where the hell were you?"

"I've been there—George and I have been there, working together, watching over you, protecting you . . . and you have seen me, I know you have. You've seen me in the shadows, on the street. You've heard me call to you. . . ."

Gaia had to admit that was true. These past few months her father had always seemed to be somewhere near her. She'd felt him, even seen him in bits and pieces, like an apparition. Or . . . was that Oliver? She'd seen him in the shadows too. Who was who? *Who the hell knows?* It was all too much to process, too confusing. Too much bullshit. Why would either one of them want to torture her like this? What were they trying to do to her?

"He saved my life," Gaia repeated quietly, talking to herself, trying to remind herself where she stood. Only she didn't really seem to know anymore.

"Gaia," her father pleaded. "You have to listen to what I'm telling you. My whole purpose for living has been to save your life. When that neo-Nazi punk CJ had you targeted in his sights, I had to act first. I was there. Watching over you. When that bastard Twain—the Gentleman—came after you . . . I was there, too. I even warned Sam about him."

How does he know CJ? Gaia asked herself, swamped in confusion. *How does he know about David Twain? And Sam?*

But there was more.

"When that chimney fell from the Perry Street town house—that was Ella Niven's doing. She wanted you dead even then. The woman had lost her mind. I called to you as the chimney fell to keep you from harm's way. I know you heard me, Gaia."

"It was you," Gaia heard herself say. She hadn't even meant to say it out loud.

"Yes. You saw me; I knew it. And when Ella tried to shoot you, Gaia. When she put that gun to your head . . . I just thank God I was there to stop her. And I called to you. Did you hear me, Gaia? Did you hear me telling you I loved you? Tell me you saw me there. Tell me you heard me—"

"I did," Gaia stated softly, looking up at the blank white ceiling of the bathroom. She felt weak. Her head was spinning. Her anger was waning. A whole other slew of emotions was leaking out of her heart, and she was doing everything in her power to plug them back up and stick to what she knew was the truth or . . . what she thought was the truth. . . .

How could he have known all these things unless he was there? He was there every time, saving her life over and over again. How could someone so evil have saved her so many times? It didn't make any sense.

"You're lying," she said with a weak lilt in her voice, not even sure if she believed herself anymore.

"I've never lied to you, Gaia," her father stated, "and I never will. Don't you see? I had to get you on this plane to save your life. Oliver must have told you a whole pack of lies to get you to leave with him. All lies, Gaia. He's planning something. Something evil. And you are the key to that plan, the last piece of the puzzle; I know that much—"

"No more," Gaia insisted, placing her hands over her eyes and trying to shake her head clear of all this information.

She wished she could be anyplace else. Anywhere but here. She wished she could be eleven years old again, driving with her mother to gymnastics, a normal kid with a normal life. She wished she were sitting in Ed Fargo's kitchen, laughing at his lame jokes over a chocolate fix. . . .

Mostly she wished she were in Sam Moon's arms, lying safely tucked away on his creaky dorm-room bed, nestling her head between his chin and his firm shoulder.

"Gaia," her father said softly. "I know you have a million reasons not to. But right now . . . more than ever before . . . I need you to trust me."

Trust.

You know what I've learned about trust? Do you know what my *father* taught me about trust?

I'll never forget the day I was standing with my father in the backyard of our house in the Berkshires, practicing my round-house kicks. The sun was setting over the mountains, and everything was bathed in this bright golden haze.

My dad tried to teach me all the lessons he'd learned as an operative for the CIA. He taught me everything he knew about martial arts, weapons, languages—you name it.

But this one day, he just stopped in the middle of my karate lesson. He'd been on some mission, and he'd just gotten back home. I remember because I was so excited to see him, I was literally jumping up and down and squealing like a poodle . . . but I also knew something about the mission had thrown him. He seemed upset the whole day—distant, pre-occupied.

And out of the blue, he knelt down next to me—at dusk, on this perfect spring day—and he put his huge hands on my ten-year-old shoulders, and he said he was going to teach me the most important lesson of them all. The first priority for all the agents. He said that most of the guys in Langley and DC referred to it as "the Golden Rule."

"The Golden Rule, Gaia," he said. *Trust no one.*

And he repeated it just to make sure I understood.

I remember, even back then, thinking this made no sense. Because obviously I was supposed to trust *him* that "trusting no one" was the right thing to do.

But looking back on it, I'd have to say it's turned out to be a pretty accurate piece of advice. Because every time I've trusted someone, they've either died on me or betrayed me.

The people I've trusted in
chronological order:
My mother—dead.
My father—disappeared on me right
    after my mother died. Then
    turned out to be Loki,
    although . . .
Ed Fargo—now dating my archenemy,
    megabitch Heather Gannis.
Sam Moon—slept with Ella
    (although it was a mistake and
    I've forgiven him).
Mary Moss—dead.
Uncle Oliver—Well, he hasn't
    betrayed me yet, but . . .
    Sam Moon, wherever you are
right now, just know this: I
trust you. Please don't let me
down. *Please, please* don't let me
down.
    And my father . . .
    I don't know what to do. I
don't know what to think. I don't
know who to trust.
    The Golden Rule, huh?
    I hate rules. Always have.

. . . he could easily kill at least four of them right at that moment. But this was **such a waste** neither the time nor the place. Taking action would only lead to further nuisance.

The Night in Question

TOM MOORE LET GO OF EVERY MUSCLE in his body, collapsing slowly against the bathroom door, sliding his back down the door until he'd reached the floor. He could feel the weight of his daughter's back leaning against his own, barely separated by one piece of cardboard-thin plastic.

Close. As close as he could get to her.

Suddenly he could feel how exhausted he'd become in the last few hours . . . in the last five years. But he welcomed his exhaustion. It was a freedom of sorts. He was too tired to "keep his chin up," to "take it like a man," as his own father used to say to him. And that was good because he needed to let his heart be raw now. Unprotected.

Since the very moment he'd seen Katia shot, he'd felt compelled to *harden* his heart. He'd told himself it was for Gaia's sake, but he'd known in truth that it was just as much for his own. And not until this moment did he truly comprehend that his heart had been frozen for five years.

Such a waste. Gaia deserved better.

It was time to break the ice and expose his heart, regardless of whatever bruised condition it might be in. But Tom knew, once he let his heart out of its icy

41

shell, it would instantly lead him right back to where he'd left it. A place he'd sworn he'd never revisit.

"Gaia," he said, almost in a whisper. "That night . . ."

Cold, stark images and sounds flashed through his head. A steady stream of dark blood pouring from Katia's mouth as her motionless body lay on the kitchen floor. The vacant, maniacal look in his brother's eyes as he fired the gun. His daughter leaning over her dead mother, sobbing.

The sound of a gunshot in his own house echoed through his head.

"The second I heard that little noise in the kitchen, I knew what it was," Tom said.

"Don't—," Gaia started.

"No," he interrupted her. "Don't talk for a moment. Please, just listen."

Gaia remained silent.

"I knew it was Oliver," Tom went on. "I knew he'd gotten into the house. And I knew that if Oliver had come into my home again, it would only be for one reason. To kill me, Gaia. That's what he was there to do. He was in love with Katia. He was obsessed with her—with having her for himself. But Katia was in love with *me,* and he couldn't accept it. He'd already fallen so deep into his psychosis, I think his jealousy was eating away at his mind. He just wanted me dead."

Tom felt woozy and overheated. A layer of cold sweat had begun to bathe his body. But he had to go on.

"But from the moment I heard him in the house," he continued, "I couldn't have cared less what he did to me . . . I just prayed that neither one of you would get hurt. I just wanted you and your mother to be safe. . . ."

Suddenly the wave of emotion was more than he could handle. His chest became so tight that he found it difficult to breathe. There was an aching pressure behind his eyes. He knew it was his natural impulse to hold back his tears no matter how hard he had to strain. He took a deep breath and then another. He wanted nothing more than to stop reliving that night. He wished he could scrape it from his memory permanently. But he knew Gaia needed to hear it. And he also knew he needed to say it.

"I tried to protect you, Gaia. . . ."

And then he was crying. He despised crying. He'd always thought it was weak and useless, self-indulgent. He hadn't even let himself cry that night. Instead he'd gone numb, blank, shut down. Of course, that was exactly why he couldn't let it happen again. He let himself cry as he spoke.

"I held you down under the table," he said, choking on his own words, "but I had to protect Katia, too. . . . It all happened so quickly, I couldn't even . . . I stepped into the kitchen, and Oliver had me in his sights . . . but Katia stepped between us—I think she thought she could reason with him, I think she thought she could stop it all from happening, but he'd already pulled the trigger, Gaia . . . he'd already pulled the trigger. . . ."

Tom had always assumed that when the day finally came, *this* day, when he allowed himself to break down about that night—to sit on the floor and sob like a baby . . . that at least there would be someone to hold him, to help him through it. But there was no one. No friend, no counselor of any kind. And his daughter was still silent behind a locked door. The sadness weighed him down, crushing him. He forced himself to speak again.

"Gaia . . . that night, Oliver did so much more than just kill your mother. He killed our happiness. *Yours and mine.* He killed the notion of happiness for us both for all these years. I only left that night because I thought it would make you safe. I thought as long as I was nowhere near you, then you couldn't possibly end up like Katia. Standing in the line of fire. But I was *wrong*, Gaia. I was wrong to leave you. I knew that from the moment . . ."

He stopped himself midsentence. Because he wanted to be as honest with himself as he was being with Gaia.

"I've always known it," he said, finally, shaking his head with a deep punishing self-hatred. "Somewhere, in some corner of my mind, I've always known it was the wrong thing to do. And I'm praying that you can forgive me because . . . I am so sorry. Please. Please give me the chance to take care of you again. To be with you again. To protect you. I won't let you down again, Gaia. Just give us a chance to be happy, to know what it is to be happy. Because I haven't been happy. Not without you. Not without you . . ."

Tom sat quietly and let the tears stream down his face. There was no sound on the other side of the door. Gaia had no response. So it truly was too late. His sins had been too much to forgive. He hadn't realized until that moment just how much he'd resigned himself in the last five years to never knowing true happiness again. He wondered how he'd be able to move successfully through another day in his life after this one. He was quite sure he could not.

And then she opened the door.

GAIA LOOKED DOWN AT HER FATHER.

Better Than a Lie Detector.

For a moment he seemed almost frightened. He just sat there with his eyes wide open, waiting for her to speak.

But she didn't. And until the moment arrived, she didn't know what she would do. Five long years had passed. Five long years of ducking that night, ducking every issue . . . ducking the man whom she thought—

She crouched down to the floor and hugged him.

She hugged him with everything that was in her—every ounce of strength, every kind of emotion, every wasted particle of rage. And they sat on the rugged industrial airplane carpeting and cried.

"Thank you," he whispered through his tears, his arms wrapped tightly around her shoulders.

"It's okay, Dad," she heard herself whisper.

She understood now. Nobody was that good of an actor. Certainly not her uncle. Certainly not Ella. Her father had suffered as much as she had; in some ways, he'd suffered more. She'd heard it. Living on gut instinct for so long, surviving for survival's sake, she'd developed a keen sense for dishonesty. Her brain was better than a lie detector. Sometimes it failed her, of course. But she knew it wasn't now. She knew it.

"It's okay," she repeated—not even caring for the moment how cheesy it sounded, not caring that she'd suddenly fallen right smack in the middle of one of those "Reunited" episodes of *Sally Jessy Raphael* or *Oprah*. It didn't matter if this moment was cheesier than the entire state of Wisconsin.

Because Gaia was happy. She was truly happy—

Yet one thought was lingering there.

"Wait a minute," she said, breaking their embrace. "If you picked me up at the airport . . . then where's Oliver?"

Tom paused for a moment. He seemed to be looking for the most appropriate answer. Finally he gave Gaia his reply.

"He was supposed to catch a plane, too. But I think he might miss it."

THERE WAS NO EXPRESSION ON LOKI'S

Smug Little Half Smile

face. Not a hint of the rage. Not a hint of the humiliation that was burning up the lining of his stomach. He wouldn't give his captors the satisfaction. With all his will, he ignored the metal handcuffs that sliced through his wrists, that cut off his circulation. He ignored the shackles on his ankles—the ones that had forced him to walk in that emasculating shuffle from the terminal to an unmarked black minivan . . . escorted by those plebeian FBI agents with their fifty-dollar suits and their ridiculous aviator sunglasses.

A nuisance, he told himself. *Nothing but a pitiful*

little nuisance. They must be so proud of themselves right now. How very pathetic.

Indeed, the eight federal agents that now surrounded him inside the van—three in the seat in back of him, three in front of him, and one on either side— all seemed quite pleased with themselves. They all had the same smug little half smile on their faces. Surely they were each reliving what had just become the crowning achievement of their careers in law enforcement: the moment they'd ambushed Loki in a giant circle at gate 17B, wielding a plethora of automatic weapons, commanding him to place his arms behind his back—then wrestling him to the ground as they read him his rights, with the most egregiously unnecessary use of force.

Ah, yes. The surprise capture of the deadly and infamous Loki.

Obviously he had made a small miscalculation at some point. Someone leaked his plans for the flight with Gaia to the Bureau, or perhaps to the Agency. He made a mental note to himself to find that person and kill him or her in as painful a manner as possible.

"You comfortable, Loki?" the agent to his left asked.

The other agents laughed.

Loki dug his fingernails deep into his palms and bit down on his tongue. He would memorize their names. Forty-eight hours from now, by which time he was sure to be free, he could kill them, too. They were such fools to think they had any kind of power over him. Such shortsighted fools.

"Hey, Loki," one of the men behind him whispered, "can I just make a suggestion? Next time you *don't* wanna get caught, you might wanna steer clear of big public places like airports, Central Park, and—oh, yeah—New York City."

Loki knew he could easily kill at least four of them right at that moment. But this was neither the time nor the place. Taking action would only lead to further nuisance. Instead he kept that same vacant glaze over his face as they sped down the Belt Parkway toward his incarceration.

Patience, he told himself. *All in due time.*

I'll happily watch all these bastards rot in hell for this—believing that their adolescent fraternity-house minds could possibly outwit me. They are lackeys, peons. Obviously there was something else at work. I'm quite sure my brother played some role in this fiasco. Oh, yes. Quite sure. I imagine he's probably made contact with Gaia by now. I imagine he's already started filling her head with puerile lies.

That self-righteous fool stole Katia from me. If he thinks that I'm going to be held captive while he tries to steal Gaia from me as well—the daughter who should have been mine, the daughter who *is* mine . . . well, then he's an even greater fool than I thought.

If Tom wants to challenge me, fine. Nothing would bring me greater pleasure than to set the past straight and erase him from existence as I'd originally intended.

No one can keep me from Gaia.
No one.

Unfortunately, I realize now that I let my feelings for her cloud my judgment. Of course I should have taken the private jet, but I wanted so much for Gaia to feel at ease with me. I wanted her to feel that we were simply an uncle and his niece off to Europe.

I miscalculated. It was too much public exposure. Too great a risk.

If only we could eliminate the heart from the human experience. Imagine how smoothly all things would run. And if my plans are to be successful, I must harden my heart from now on. I must check and double-check that it plays no part in my actions from this point on. I must listen only to logic.

What he felt most,
lying there shirtless
and dripping and
goddamn
brazilian
staring at the
ceiling, could **rain**
only be **forest**
described as a
serious jolt of . . .
well, manliness.

KNOCK KNOCK KNOCK—

New Favorite Human Being

"Open up," Detective Bernard called from behind the door. "We know you're in there."

Sam wrapped the covers over his head.

He couldn't believe this. They were already back—a mere two hours after that first rude awakening. Didn't they have any *other* crimes to solve?

"Mr. Moon!" the other one shouted, suddenly dropping any modicum of civility. "Open this goddamn door!"

The shouting was no good. The last thing Sam needed was screaming cops echoing through his hall in the middle of the evening. It wouldn't be long before he had a mass audience of gossip-starved hung-over sophomores piling into his suite. Besides, he was a little old to be hiding under the covers. He ripped the sheets away once again and stumbled to the door as quickly as possible, before there was time for another high-decibel threat. He flipped the lock on the door and whipped it open.

"Yes! Jesus, all right!" he barked. "I thought I answered all your questions!"

The detectives gave him the once-over.

"You wanna put some pants on, son?" Reilly finally asked with a judgmental glare.

Great. Sam had forgotten to throw on his T-shirt this time—leaving him stark naked except for a pair of flimsy boxers. Now they probably thought he was a pervert, too. He swiveled around and quickly sifted through the piles of clothes in his tenement-size dorm room, grabbing a wrinkled pair of khakis and a purple NYU sweatshirt.

The detectives wasted no time making themselves at home. They immediately began pawing through Sam's possessions and cracking open drawers in his desk and his dresser. For chrissake—was that *legal?* Didn't he have any rights? And what on earth were they looking for?

"So, do you know of any reason someone would want to kill Suarez?" Reilly asked, flipping through one of Sam's biology notebooks.

"You already asked me that," Sam grumbled, grabbing the notebook out of his hands.

"*Chill,* homeboy," Reilly said with a grin.

"You know, we checked with that movie theater, Sam," Bernard stated as he examined Sam's CD collection. "Did you know there was no foreign movie playing that night? Isn't that weird? Maybe you went to another theater, huh?"

Sam's stomach twisted itself into a knot. Once again he wanted to slap himself on the head for that stupid movie alibi. Why hadn't he just said he was at the library or something?

"Maybe I did . . . or I didn't. Maybe. I—I don't know," he stammered inanely.

"You know what, Sammy?" Bernard snapped, sitting down on the bed. "I'm gettin' sick of playing nice. And I'm gettin' sick and tired of your attitude. I think you're lying. I think you're a liar."

Sam wondered if the burst of fear had shown through in his eyes. Did they know something about Ella?

"I'm not a liar," he murmured, making a conscious effort to reveal as little as possible with his facial expression.

"Bullshit," Bernard snapped. "Everything you're giving me is bullshit!"

"What are you talking about?" Sam cried. "What—"

"What *do* you know, Moon? The guy was right across the hall, for crying out loud. Were you there when it happened or not?"

"I wasn't there!" Sam insisted.

"You really think I'm buying your routine?" Bernard grimaced. "You overprivileged college kids think you're so damn smart. What, you think me and my partner here are too dumb to see what's goin' on? You think it's floatin' right over our doughnut-eatin' heads?"

"Overprivileged?" Sam asked, baffled. Was that what they were so pissed about? Jesus. "You don't know me. You don't know a damn thing about me. I've worked my ass off—"

"*Wah,*" Bernard interrupted. "You poor thing. Is that why you did it? Was the pressure too much for you?"

"Did it?" Sam retorted, forgetting his fear and giving in to anger. "Did *what?*"

55

"Why'd you kill Suarez?" Reilly barked.

Sam's jaw dropped. His vision darkened. He was no longer conscious of anything but this room, this *moment*. All the blood drained from his face and seemed to pool in his feet. He didn't even know what he was feeling: It was something beyond fear. *My God. They think*—

"Reilly, we seem to have struck a nerve," Bernard said with a smile.

"I didn't kill Mike," Sam stated, his voice quavering.

"Well, that's not how we see it right now—"

"I didn't kill *Mike!*" Sam hollered.

"Bingo!" Reilly sang out, startling Sam and causing both him and Bernard to look over at him by the desk. He was holding something up in his hand triumphantly.

A syringe. One of Sam's syringes for his insulin.

"You like to keep extra syringes hanging around, Sam?" Reilly demanded.

Bernard smiled with deep satisfaction.

Sam didn't get it. He couldn't even comprehend what had happened in the last two minutes. He'd been running scared from the cops, and he hadn't even known how scared he should have been. He knew he was a potential witness, but a potential suspect? How did they come up with that? His mouth felt like he'd just stuffed a bag of cotton down his throat. His head felt like a giant squid had just rapped its tentacles around it and tried to squeeze out his brain. He had to start talking. He had to start talking fast.

"I'm a diabetic," Sam explained, trying to keep his eyes from revealing that he was in deer-in-headlights mode. "That's for my insulin. I inject myself—"

"So, then, you'd say you're good with needles?" Reilly asked with a smug grin as he pulled a Ziploc bag out of his pocket and dropped the syringe into it.

"Yes, but—"

"That's all we need for an arrest," Bernard growled. "The syringe was in plain sight." He pulled a pair of handcuffs from his belt. Before Sam could process what was happening, Bernard had grabbed his arm, twisted it behind his back, and squeezed his wrist as if he were planning to break it off. A sting of pain shot all the way up to Sam's shoulder. Bernard flipped the right handcuff onto his wrist, instantly cutting off his circulation.

"You have the right to remain silent," he announced. "Anything you say can and will be used against you in a court of law. . . ."

"What the hell are you doing?" Sam demanded. This couldn't really be happening. There was no way this could really be happening—

"You have the right to an attorney," Bernard went on, snapping the other cuff on Sam's other wrist.

This can't be happening, Sam kept repeating inside his head. *This can't be happening. It's a nightmare. That's all—*

"If you do not wish—"

Sam's door crashed open, cutting off Bernard in midsentence.

Some guy Sam had never seen before was standing there, dressed in jogging shorts and an NYU sweatshirt. His clothes were drenched in sweat, and his straight jet black hair was hanging over his bright blue eyes. The guy's gaze swept the room, his face twisting in a scowl.

"What's going on here?" he demanded, staring at the cops as if they were insane.

"Stay cool, Tom Cruise," Bernard said, pushing Sam toward the door, Reilly following. "Your buddy here is just getting arrested."

But the guy stood his ground at the doorway. Sam caught a glimpse of the suite outside his room—and just as he'd feared, it was inundated with curious sophomores, all craning their necks to see inside. Blood rushed to Sam's face.

"Arrested? You're a cop?" the stranger asked.

Bernard rolled his eyes and pulled out his badge with his free hand.

"Detective Bernard, NYPD. Who the hell are you?"

"I'm Josh Kendall," he stated, brazenly looking Bernard in the eye. "I'm the new resident adviser on this floor. And maybe since I'm so new, maybe since I'm just sort of getting used to the way things are run . . . I'm not quite sure what's supposed to happen. But I'm pretty sure I can't have you barging in here and just cuffing one of my guys unless you've got a warrant. Do you have a warrant?"

Sam twisted his neck back at Bernard and Reilly. They had no response.

"You've gotta be kidding me," Bernard mumbled under his breath. "What are you, twenty, twenty-two? I got crap-stained Skivvies older than you."

"Be that as it may," Josh said, "you still haven't answered my question. Do you have a warrant?"

Everyone waited silently for the answer: Sam, Josh, and the pack of kids trying to catch the whole show.

"No," Bernard finally admitted. "But the syringe was in—"

"No warrant?" Josh shouted, his disbelief laden heavily with sarcasm. He turned to Sam. "Did they touch anything in here?"

Sam could barely muster a nod. Who was this guy, anyway? And why was he putting himself out to save Sam's ass? He hadn't heard about any new RA. Wasn't the university supposed to notify students about developments like this? On the other hand, maybe NYU tried to notify him, but he'd been so preoccupied and paranoid and distracted that he hadn't noticed—

"I can't believe this." Josh groaned, shaking his head. "Do the words *police misconduct* mean anything to you? I mean, didn't you learn anything from the OJ trial? Take those cuffs off him and come back here when you've got a warrant. Unless you want some real trouble. Any first-year law student could get you guys kicked off the force for this, you know that?"

Detective Bernard looked like his blood pressure had just shot up into the danger zone. He started to lean in toward Josh.

"You little—"

"Do it," Josh encouraged him. "That'll be the kicker in court. Police brutality. Be my guest."

Bernard looked at Josh, then back at Sam. He cracked his neck once to the right and once to the left, obviously trying to control his temper. It was right there on his flaccid, ugly face: He wanted nothing more than to belt Josh in the gut and haul him downtown. But instead he pulled his key from his belt and unlocked Sam's handcuffs.

"Merry Christmas," he murmured, his nose about an inch from Sam's. Then he turned to his partner. "Come on. This place stinks, anyway."

Reilly followed him out, and in seconds—miracle of miracles—Sam Moon was a free man again. The suite hadn't cleared, though. It was still full of sophomores, including his other roommate, Brendan Moss. They were all still staring at him as if he were a criminal. But he didn't care right now. Right now, all he cared about was that those two cops were gone.

"You all right?" Josh asked.

Sam looked at him. No, he was far from all right.

He was confused, scared, shaky. He was still in utter disbelief that he could possibly be wanted for Mike's murder. But he was far too grateful to talk about any of that right now. All he wanted to do was give his new RA and new favorite human being a huge hug.

"I'm okay," he said. "Thanks, man. I have no idea how I could possibly repay you for this."

"It's no big deal," Josh replied, slapping Sam's shoulder. "If I ever need a favor, I'll let you know. . . ." He left his sentence open, clearly waiting to hear Sam's name.

"Sam. Sam Moon."

"Josh," he said, shaking Sam's hand firmly. "I'm staying in Mike Suarez's room. Just temporarily—until the RA single at the end of the hall is ready for me. I hope that's not weird. . . ."

"No, no," Sam said. "That's cool. That's great."

Josh peered at him. "Correct me if I'm wrong, but you're looking very freaked out, dude."

"I am a little, yeah," Sam admitted, running his hands through his hair, trying in vain to shake off the last ten minutes. "I can't say I've ever been arrested before."

"I think you need some coffee," Josh suggested. "Is there a decent place around here to get coffee?"

Sam tried to force himself to breathe normally. Coffee with Josh sounded a hell of a lot better than lying back down in his bed and thinking about what had just happened. Contrary to what he'd thought just the night before, he was nowhere *near* being out of the woods. No, if he'd thought he was out of the woods, then apparently he'd walked out of the woods and into a goddamn Brazilian rain forest. Yes. A good cup of coffee was exactly what Sam needed. Something to wake him up from this nightmare.

"WE'RE GONNA DO ONE MORE, ED.

Do you think you can do one more?"

The sweat was pouring down Ed Fargo's body, leaving a puddle of water on his wheelchair-accessible bed big enough

Grandpappy in Texas

to fill the average kiddie swimming pool. He knew his face must be beet red. Sure, it was the very first physical therapy session since his operation——but he was seriously considering making it his last. How could he be so exhausted from leg lifts when he couldn't even feel his legs?

Brian, the physical therapist (who clearly moonlighted as a WWF wrestler), was staring down at Ed with intense wide-eyed anticipation.

No way, Ed thought. *Absolutely not. I can't take*

another one. Please don't make me, scary physical thera-pist who may break a folding chair over me if I don't. Please don't make me do another leg lift.

But that wasn't how he answered. That wasn't how good old Shred would respond to a challenge. He'd sworn to himself that he'd work his ass off for this. Even if he couldn't actually feel his ass.

"Uh-huh," Ed grunted through his pain.

"Yes!" Brian growled, throwing up his arms and jerking his fists backward toward his ultrapumped chest. The guy's neck was a tree trunk. "You da man, *Eddie!* You da man!"

Ed realized something at that moment. Something pretty scary, in fact. In a totally twisted way, Brian was a lot like Shred used to be: full of testosterone, relatively fearless, and mildly insane. (Even scarier was that Ed thought of his former per-sona, "Shred," as a different person. But that was another story—and one that would probably take years of therapy to fix.)

"Let's go, baby!" Brian hollered. "One more! One more for your grandpappy in Texas!"

"What?" Ed grunted. He had no grandpappy in Texas.

"Or whatever, dude," Brian, shouted, cradling Ed's left knee in one hand and his ankle in the other. "One more for Freddy Durst, dude! Bizkit rocks!"

"What?" Ed squeaked as Brian began to lift his

creaky leg, sending lightning bolts of agony up his spine.

"Do it for Tyler and Perry, dude! Seventy-two years old and still kickin' it! Do it for Aerosmith, Eddie. *I want you to rock like freakin' thunder, baby!*"

Ed could have spent hours trying to dissect Brian's bizarre encouragement tactics, but any and all thought processes were interrupted by the agony stabbing through Ed's lower back as Brian bent his knee.

"*Uuuugh*," Ed groaned with supreme effort, trying to hold his body together.

"*And* . . . seven," Brian announced, finally letting Ed's leg back down on his bed to rest. He and Ed both let out a long sigh.

Seven leg lifts.

That's what Ed had spent the last forty-five minutes doing? Seven measly leg lifts. Pathetic. He was sure he'd done at least twenty. It was going to be a long, long road. A road that led quite possibly, and most likely, nowhere.

"Yes, dude," Brian screamed with a maniacal grin, pounding Ed on the shoulder. "That was freakin' beautiful, Ed. You're Hercules, Eddie. You're the man. I'm gonna check in with your folks, and I'll catch you tomorrow. We're goin' for ten, baby. Maybe fifteen! Peace!"

Brian slammed the door, leaving Ed soaking in his own juices.

And then something very strange happened.

The pain disappeared from Ed's body. What he felt

most, lying there shirtless and dripping and staring at the ceiling, could only be described as a serious jolt of . . . well, manliness. He felt empowered. As insane as Brian was, he was absolutely right. Ed was a man. For the first time in years he didn't just remember what it felt like to have power; he could actually feel it. He could feel the blood rushing through every part of his body as a whole. Not just half of him. Every part of him.

Images started racing through his head—images of him and Heather Gannis doing anything and everything they wanted. Yes, they were already back together, but they still hadn't really gotten very far in this new incarnation of their relationship.

Of course, Ed still hadn't told Heather about the surgery. He'd made up a lame excuse about being at his aunt's house. But now that it was done, telling her was the only thing on his mind. The possibilities . . . the numerous possibilities . . .

Physical memories were running through him, starting at his hands and moving through the rest of his body . . . memories of what it felt like to be with Heather. Memories of being tangled up and pressed against her on the beach in the middle of the night, when all they could hear were their own quick breathing and the steady rhythm of the waves. Nothing had ever felt so good in his life.

Then he flashed forward to the present—struck by

a vivid image of himself, lifting Heather off his lap and carrying her to the bed. . . .

Suddenly he realized that he couldn't even remember if he was taller than Heather. Well . . . of course he was. But what about other people? Was he taller than Gaia Moore? He'd been in the chair long before the first time he and Gaia had met. He wondered . . . if they were standing close to each other, face-to-face, would they look straight into each other's eyes . . . or would she have to tilt her head upward to see his face? Or if he held her, where would his hands press against her? Would she wrap her arms around his waist or behind his neck? If she were lying on top of him right now in bed, their legs entangled, would her head fall on his chest or—

"Whoa," Ed mumbled out loud. What was he thinking? Obviously testosterone, as it has been known to do, had seized Ed's brain for a moment. But he quickly regained his senses. It was just a momentary brain lapse, that was all.

He was completely over Gaia . . . in *that way.*

I just need to see Heather, he told himself. *Even a few days is way too long.*

From: shred@alloymail.com
To: heathery@alloymail.com
Re: Return of the Mack
Time: 12:32 P.M.

Heather,

I am *back* from my aunt's house. And I am *stoked*. I'm taking you to dinner at a trendy, totally overpriced spot of your choosing, and I'm telling you some unbelievable news. News that is not to be believed.

I mean, it actually would be wiser not to believe it, but . . . .

I'll explain later.

Can't wait to see you.

—Shred

"CAN WE NOT TALK ABOUT THIS
now, please?" Heather's father grumbled. He stabbed his plastic fork into a white cardboard container of beef lo mein. The carton seemed to be the only place he was comfortable focusing his gaze.

Poor Rich People

"When exactly do you want to talk about it?" her mother snapped, throwing her chopsticks down on her soggy container of mu shu vegetables. "You never want to talk about it!"

Heather tried to tune them out. Unfortunately, given the volume of their voices, it was impossible.

"Oh, for chrissake." Her father groaned. "It's Phoebe's one night home for the week. I want us to have a nice family dinner. And I want to talk about nice things. Happy things."

"And which things would they be?" her mother replied, glaring at him. "That you have no job and no apparent prospects? Or that we're flat broke?"

Nice. Really nice. Well, that confirmed it: The dining room had become the most depressing room in the house by far. It was the weekly site of "family time," when her sister—still looking extremely pale and sickly from her bout with anorexia—would visit home from her recovery center and eat an "inexpensive dinner." That was the new favorite word around the house, the catchphrase: "inexpensive." In order for anyone to do anything, it had to be "inexpensive." Of course it did. Her father had lost his job, and Phoebe's care had drained her family's savings. No . . . the dining room was beyond depressing. It was mortifying.

Heather had to keep reminding herself that this was, in fact, *her* life and not the life of some fictional movie character. Her eyes floated over to a family picture from just a year ago that sat in a bright silver frame on the mantel of the dining-room fireplace. It was a shot of the four of them from when they'd gone skiing in Aspen just last year. Each of them was grinning joyfully, all swaddled in their red or blue down coats, with their thick white scarves and their flushed red cheeks.

That's my family, she told herself. *These people are just a bunch of bad actors in the Lifetime TV version of my life. "People in Crisis: The Heather Gannis Story."*

Heather's dad threw his food down on the dining-room table and grabbed Phoebe's skeletal hand.

"Maybe we could be happy about the fact that our beautiful daughter is recovering from her illness?" he growled. "Wouldn't you say that's a happy thing? That she's eating again?"

Heather looked at her sister. Recovering? That was a nice way of putting it. Phoebe's skin was still almost translucent, the blue veins bulging throughout her body. She was pinching a rubbery piece of steamed broccoli between the thumb and index finger of her available hand, holding it as if it were some disgusting worm she'd just dissected in biology class.

"She's going back to Chelsea tonight," her father hissed, "so let's enjoy these few hours, all right?"

Phoebe's recovery center was this oddly tasteful upscale town house in Chelsea, filled with Oriental rugs and pricey knickknacks. Heather didn't even want to imagine what her parents were paying to keep her there. Then again, up until the last few weeks, Heather had never even thought for a moment about what her parents were paying for anything. It had never been much of an issue before. At all.

"Well, would you like her to stay in the recovery center?" her mother asked. Her voice was dripping with sarcasm. "If you won't look for a job, I don't see why—"

"I'm looking for a job!" he shouted. "And if I need to find the money, then goddamn it, I'll find the—"

"Stop it!" Phoebe interrupted, yanking her frail hand from her father's grasp and slamming it on the table. "I know I'm skinny, but I'm not invisible. I'm sitting right here, so stop talking about me like I'm not. I'm sorry that I'm so expensive, I really am. I'm sorry. . . ." Her voice broke. Tears streamed down her cheeks.

"May I be excused?" Heather asked. She couldn't take this melodrama for another second. It was too painful—not to mention too pathetic. Family dinner was most definitely a bust. She was half tempted to mention what Ed had told her the other night at dinner, that he would always take care of her and her family . . . but no. She didn't even know if that was true or not. Yes, she trusted Ed. Of course she did. But sincerity didn't pay the bills. Besides, Ed's parents might not be thrilled with the idea of Ed's helping the Gannis family. Particularly given her and Ed's tempestuous past . . .

Her father glared at her but finally nodded.

Heather placed her hand gently on her sister's shoulder and mouthed the words: "I'll come visit you tomorrow."

Her sister tried to smile through her tears. Then Heather bolted for her bedroom. It felt a bit like having to reach the toilet before throwing up. *Money,* she thought as she slammed her door and collapsed on her canopy brass bed in tears. *It all comes down to money.*

It was almost funny. She had been trying all week to convince herself that money couldn't buy happiness, but even if that was true (which she doubted), the lack of money sure seemed to ensure unhappiness.

She glanced over at her answering machine, hoping. Praying.

Nothing. Ed still hadn't called. He hadn't called once since he'd gone away.

Where are you, Ed?

If she could just go over to Ed's place tonight. Or why just go to his house? Maybe she could start a new life with Ed in Aruba or Antigua or something. Just the two of them on the beach. Maybe some fine dining . . . maybe a fine hotel—

The phone rang.

Heather nearly burst out laughing. It was like a miracle from God. Just when she needed him the most . . . wow. She seemed to be living one cliché after another. But this one she welcomed with all her heart. She leaped from her bed and snagged the cordless phone off the recharger.

"Ed, you *jerk*," she cried with a gleeful sniffle. "Where have you been?"

"Oh my God . . . chill."

Heather's heart sank—instantly. She almost felt like she'd been punched.

It wasn't Ed. It was Megan Stein. The girl laughed, her voice breaking up on a cell phone. "What's your damage, Heather?"

Heather hated it when Megan quoted from *Heathers*. Megan never seemed to understand that the entire point of that particular Winona vehicle was to expose the beautiful people for the petty, insecure, conformist losers that they were. But Megan still wanted to be a "Heather." She thrived on privilege and superiority—and, of course, dissing the people who had neither.

"Hey, Meegs," Heather uttered with as much normalcy as she could muster. "I was expecting someone else—"

"Okay." Megan's voice cut her off, echoing through the distant land of cell phone. "I am currently in a cab with Tina and Shauna, and we have a message for you."

Heather heard Megan mumble something to the other girls. And then, with the phone clearly pulled away from her mouth: "Ready? One, two, three . . . *loserrrrr!*" the three girls shouted in unison, followed by waves of self-congratulatory laughter. Heather cringed as she pulled the phone away from her ear.

"Loser, where *are* you?" Megan went on.

"I'm home," Heather answered, frowning. "You called *me*, remember?"

"Um . . . duh," Megan replied. She giggled again. "Look, we want you to come meet us at Serendipity for hot chocolates."

"I can't tonight," Heather answered automatically. "I . . . I'm having dinner with my parents." She swallowed. She wasn't sure how much longer she could keep blowing off her friends due to lack of funds. But the simple fact was, she couldn't afford any of the usual activities—not even a hot chocolate. Nothing that her friends wanted to do seemed to qualify as "inexpensive."

There was a brief silence.

"What's your problem, Heather?" Megan finally asked, with genuine annoyance. "Are you avoiding us or what?"

Heather opened her mouth, then closed it. She was getting so sick of coming up with stupid little stories to avoid her friends. But there was nothing she could do. She couldn't tell them she was poor. They wouldn't believe her, for starters.

"I can't tonight," she repeated.

"Fine. Whatever."

Click.

"Hello?" Heather called into her phone. "Meegs?"

Nothing. There was a dead silence on the other end.

Well, she thought, slamming her phone back down on the recharger. Her throat tightened. Her eyes began to sting. *Could my life possibly get any worse? My family is screwed. My friends hate me. Ed is . . .*

Maybe he'd e-mailed?

Heather hopped into her desk chair and jabbed the power button on her computer, holding her breath as it whirred to life. *Come on, come on . . .* grabbing her mouse, she clicked into her e-mail. She made a decision, fighting back tears: If there was no mail from Ed, she would have to start planning her life as a runaway right now. . . .

But there it was: the little e-mail icon with shred@alloymail.com in the sender column.

Joy washed over her—a thirty-foot-high, hurricane-style wave of joy.

From: heatherg@alloymail.com
To: shred@alloymail.com
Re: Return of the Mack
Time: 7:42 P.M.

Ed,

You have no *idea* how happy I am that you're back. You have no idea how much I've missed you.

I can't wait to see you. I mean, I *really* can't wait to see you. And I can't wait to hear your news!

What I'm trying to say here is *yes*, I would be most honored to accompany you to any number of trendy overpriced restaurants (although I do have a particular one in mind).

I'll tell you when and where.

And just in case you don't remember what I look like, I'll be the stunning brunette in black velvet.

I can't wait. Did I say that already?

Love,

Heather

P.S. I know how silly this looks, and I know how stupid I sound. Please forgive me. I'm just really, really psyched to see you.

Okay.

So, about my being fortune's hamster . . .

I may have been a little extreme.

That is to say: I may not have considered, as we're trained to do in many disciplines ranging from physics to the martial arts, the potential for unforeseen circumstances.

That is to say: It seems that by some twist of bizarro unexplainable planetary misalignment or something, there seems to be this little . . . window—this little heretofore never-seen escape hatch whereby I seem to have landed in a sort of twilight zone where there's, like, this alternate universe, containing in it some sort of matter-antimatter reversal, causing a certain unexplainable, unidentifiable phenomenon that can only be defined as—

I'll stop.

I can't explain it away. I just have to say it. I'm just going to say it. But I don't want

G
A
I
A

to say it. If I say it, it dies,
and I don't want it to die.

These last three days with my
father, I've been . . . happy.

Yes, I've been confused. And
enraged. And sad. And hurt. And
thinking a lot about my mother. And
thinking a lot about Uncle Oliver,
of course. Or Loki. Or whoever. But
what matters most is that I've
looked into my father's eyes. I've
seen the truth. And I know we have
to be very careful right now. We've
got to stay inconspicuous until my
dad gets a confirmation that the
FBI ambush was successful and
Oliver is securely behind bars.
Apparently prison isn't much of a
problem for Oliver. That's part of
the reason we went straight from
Germany to Paris, via the train.

Paris is even more beautiful
than I imagined.

Not that we've been getting
out much. Mostly we've just been
trying to catch up on five years
of missing out and trying to forget five years of hell.

She felt a burst of adrenaline— that old familiar sensation she hadn't felt **shiny** since she'd **black** left New York . . . **metal** the one that came instead of fear.

GAIA HAD LEARNED A GREAT MANY

Constantly Reinventing Itself

life-altering facts in the last seventy-two hours. She'd quickly realized that it was best just to prioritize—to shuffle the nonessential information to the bottom of the pile. So at the moment she was only concentrating on three points:

1. She still had a father who loved her (and wanted her around).

2. She never wanted to leave his side again.

3. She wanted to live in Paris for the rest of her life. Actually, she made that last decision on the fourth day—when her father decided to get out a little. He took her on a grand tour that wound up at the Musée d'Orsay, a museum just across the road from the Seine. She couldn't get over this city. In a weird way, Paris was like New York. Only a lot more beautiful. All the buildings looked like palaces. But both cities seemed slightly above the rest of the world—as if everyone and everything in them was more real, more genuine.

She was especially reminded of New York in the Latin Quarter. Quai St. Michel felt so much like some of the more secluded parts of Bleecker Street or West

Fourth—those narrow little streets where you were just as likely to find a falafel joint next to a quaint French bistro. But in the case of the Latin Quarter, there were no cars to get in the way. The streets of Quai St. Michel existed only for the people, making it so much more human, so much more intimate.

And there was also something special about Paris that New York lacked. Gaia could only describe it as a sort of "life force." New York was filled with beauty and variety and culture, but somehow it always felt like it was deteriorating, always fighting to resist this inevitable decay. It had to be constantly reinventing itself, or it would die. The buildings of the rich became the hollow crack dens of the poor. The grand subways of the past became the graffiti-covered relics of the present. New York was always starting from scratch with something just a little more ugly and gritty.

But in Paris, it almost seemed like the river Seine was some sort of fountain of youth. Even though the city was much older than New York, everything had a strange, ageless quality. And it felt truly *alive*. The cobbled roads and cafés were breathing. Nowhere was this feeling more powerful, though, than at the Arc de Triomphe—the real Arc de Triomphe. The miniature version in Washington Square Park had marked the one place where she felt at home . . . under its shadow, at the chess tables, with her buddy Zolov and Mr. Haq and the finest freaks New York had to offer. It had become the center of her universe. But the real Arc in Paris made the miniature version in the park seem like a papier-mâché toy.

Slowly but surely, Gaia was beginning to feel like Paris itself. She was beginning to feel more alive, more significant. She wasn't even tired by the time they reached the Musée d'Orsay—even though darkness had fallen, and they'd been walking all day. The building had once been a huge railway station, which made it an even more stunning museum—huge and vaulted.

Tom had brought Gaia here with a specific purpose in mind. Katia had always loved the impressionists, and this particular museum housed more of their works than any other in Paris. Tom wanted Gaia to experience them in person.

Any time Gaia learned of something that had given her mother pleasure or had great meaning for her, she embraced it instantly, hoping to make it her own. Even if Gaia couldn't bring back her mother's life, she could at least bring back her ideas and emotions. And approaching this glorious building from a side street, with Tom guiding her gaze, her mother felt more present than she ever had in the last five years. The crisp Paris night and dark indigo sky only added to her intoxication—as did the warm street lanterns reflecting in rows of glowing gold on the river.

"What else did Mom like?" Gaia found herself asking. "I mean, aside from impressionist paintings?"

Her father smiled. "You don't remember?"

Gaia shrugged. "I remember some things," she answered, flashing back to the smell of stuffed cabbage and stroganoff wafting through the house as her mother hummed a Russian folk song. "But tell me more."

"She loved . . . the second movement—"

"Of the Sibelius violin concerto; I remember *that*." Gaia snorted good-naturedly, as if it were the most obvious thing in the world.

"She loved to watch you do gymnastics," he murmured. "She loved the—"

He was cut short by a piercing cry for help.

The shrill sound sliced through the night. Gaia's smile instantly faded. She felt a burst of adrenaline— that old familiar sensation she hadn't felt since she'd left New York . . . the one that came instead of fear. Tom stepped in front of her, but Gaia ducked under his arms.

Up ahead in a lone shaft of light was an elderly woman on her knees, having a violent tug-of-war for her purse. A tall lanky man in a black overcoat was yanking at the handbag, but Gaia's eyes flashed to another man who was coming up from behind them. As his hand came from the pocket of his coat Gaia saw the brief glint of black shiny metal.

"Gaia," Tom whispered urgently. "Careful. It could be a trap. Oliver's minions are everywhere. . . ."

But she was already breaking free and bursting into a full-throttle run. If it was a trap, she'd deal with it.

"*Laissez-lu tranquille!*" she screamed, demanding that the two muggers leave the old woman alone.

They both turned.

And that was all the extra time she needed.

Gaia's feet left the ground. She plowed the gun toter to the ground with a full flying tackle, then used her momentum to continue rolling in a graceful somersault. The gun clattered to the pavement. She snatched it up. At that moment the other one—a tall, bohemian-looking type with long black greased-up hair, a hideously skinny face, and a black goatee—lunged for her.

Unfortunately, he also had a knife.

No, not a knife. That thing could qualify as a machete.

But Gaia relaxed. With one effortless smooth motion she reached in for his wrist and stepped out of his way—cracking his arm over her bent knee with her right hand and simultaneously pistol whipping the back of his head with the left.

"*Aiiee!*" he cried. (Screams of pain were the same in any language.)

As he fell, Gaia deftly swiped the machete from his grasp with her free hand. He collapsed on top of his accomplice. Before either one of the poor bastards could look up from the ground, Gaia was already standing over them, the gun in her left hand, the machete in her right—gun aimed at the gun toter's head, machete an inch from the knife wielder's neck.

Both of them were whimpering. Gaia had to smile. The sound of fear. She'd never made it herself, but she recognized it well enough. Especially coming from cowards who would attack a helpless old woman.

"*Partez maintenant*," she ordered, lifting the weapons away.

Translation: *Leave now.*

She liked to keep things simple.

TOM FIGURED IT TOOK GAIA NO MORE

than four seconds to subdue both men. Both *armed* men. Once again—in spite of fear and apprehension—his heart swelled with fatherly pride. Quite simply, watching Gaia's grace and nobility in action gave him a thrill. And he was now almost ninety-nine percent certain that these men had nothing to do with Loki . . . particularly as they scampered off into the Parisian night. No, they were just a couple of unlucky muggers who'd happened to meet the wrong girl.

Gaia emptied the bullets from the gun. Tom rushed to the old woman to help her to her feet. But once she was standing, she broke from his arms and fell into Gaia's, tears streaming down her sagging weathered face.

"*Merci,*" she cried at least twenty times in a row, embracing her young heroine. "*Vous êtes un ange. Un ange!*"

You are an angel, she was saying. *An angel!*

Gaia tried to smile—but it was clear that she was terribly uncomfortable. Tom understood the reaction. She preferred to do good deeds anonymously—never for the gratitude, never for the thanks.

The old woman then turned to Tom and asked him if the "angel" was his daughter. Tom nodded. She kissed Gaia on both cheeks. But Tom noticed that Gaia wasn't only uncomfortable; something was wrong with her. Her eyelids were fluttering. In the pale light of the streetlamp her skin was deathly pale.

"Gaia?" he asked, stepping toward her.

She didn't answer. Instead her eyes rolled back in her head, and she pitched backward. The old woman let out a whimper of shock as Tom dashed forward and scooped her into his arms. He suddenly remembered his very first day of orientation as an agent, when all the trainees had been forced to do those childish "trust falls." Only now they didn't seem so childish—

"Is she all right?" the woman asked in French, aghast.

Tom scrutinized his daughter's face, holding his breath.

Gaia nodded and smiled, very faintly. "Sorry," she said with a moan. "I'll be all right in a second. Can you just hold me?"

Tom squeezed her limp body close. If she said she would be fine, then he knew that she would. She was a survivor.

"Don't worry, I've got you," he whispered. His throat clenched. "I've got you, and I'll never let you go."

"YOU DON'T UNDERSTAND," SAM

insisted, shivering in the cold Washington Square Park wind. "I can't stop thinking about her. All day. Every day. It's insane."

Mysterious Dark Secrets

"Well, I don't blame you, dude," Josh replied as he took Sam's bishop with his knight. "She sounds unbelievable. Check."

Sam blinked. "What?"

He had to laugh. He couldn't believe he'd missed it.

He surveyed the stone chessboard. Not only was Josh the guy who'd saved his ass single-handedly, he was also a damn good chess player. But at least the game wasn't totally lost. Sam's other bishop was in position to take Josh's knight. Still, his initial game plan had been ruined.

"Hees head is een the stahrs," came Zolov's thick Russian accent from the next chess table.

Sam smirked. Chess in Washington Square Park wouldn't be the same if Zolov wasn't razzing the other players or hustling chumps, his haggard, bumlike aesthetic masking the skills of a grand master. And his trusty little red Mighty Morphin Power Ranger (which sat on his table in perpetuity) didn't hurt his hustle, either. If necessary, he could always discuss potential moves with his action figure for insane effect. Of course, seeing as he was playing Mr. Haq—another regular—there was no need for any act. Zolov could just beat him, the way he usually did.

"Come on, Zolov," Sam said. "My head's not in the stars. I'm totally focused here. You know I don't mess around in a game."

"Focus?" Zolov scoffed. "How you focus when in your mind, eet just keep going 'Ceendy, Ceendy, Ceendy'—heh heh heh. . . ." Zolov let out a phlegmatic cough. Even Mr. Haq dropped his concentration to laugh in Sam's face.

"Yeah, maybe you're right," Sam admitted.

"Cindy? Who's Cindy?" Josh asked, grinning. "I thought her name was Gaia."

"I'll explain later," Sam mumbled. He and Gaia had long since given up on convincing Zolov that Cindy wasn't Gaia's name. That was just what he believed. The amazing thing was, he had also believed that Sam and Gaia were meant to be together, even before Sam and Gaia believed it. He kept telling Sam in one way or another. Then again, Sam had barely noticed; he'd been too wrapped up in Ella's insanity and Mike's murder.

If only Gaia's feelings had been as obvious to Sam back then, they wouldn't have needed to waste so much time putting themselves and each other through hell. But it had been so hard for Sam to be honest because he had still been with Heather. And Gaia . . . well . . .

She wasn't really one to express her feelings openly. It always seemed her life was too complicated, too filled with mysterious dark secrets. She was so hard to read. . . .

"Man, I miss her so much," Sam muttered to himself, shaking his head.

"Dude, you've got it bad," Josh said—but his tone was sympathetic.

"Look at heem," Zolov remarked, making Josh and Mr. Haq his audience. "He ees like loveseeck small poodle dog."

Josh laughed. So did Mr. Haq. Even Sam had to smile.

"Uh-oh," Josh suddenly muttered, peering over Sam's shoulder.

Sam turned to see what had switched Josh's mood so instantly. It was Brendan, with a couple of girls Sam had never met before. He knew they were juniors, but that was about it. A twitter of nervousness shot through him. Brendan hadn't looked at him the same since Mike's death. In fact, Brendan had avoided him.

"Brendan, what's up?' Sam asked, motioning for him to come join them.

Brendan didn't smile in return.

Sam swallowed. He knew exactly what was going on here: Brendan was suspicious. How could he really believe Sam would hurt one of his friends? "Come here," Sam called.

"No." Brendan shook his head.

Sam sighed. "Why not?"

"I . . . don't want to be seen with you."

Now Sam was pissed. "Why the hell not?"

Brendan didn't answer. The girls stared at their feet.

"Look, Brendan," Sam began. "How could you possibly think that I—"

"I know you've been acting like a psycho for weeks," Brendan interrupted. "And that's what I told them."

"Told them?" Sam's pulse picked up a beat. "Told who?"

"And I'm transferring to another dorm, Sam,"

89

Brendan stated, leaving the question unanswered, "so find yourself another roommate." With that, he and the girls turned and walked away.

Sam's heart was now pounding full throttle. Suddenly he realized how many faces were turned toward him. Suspicious faces, whispering on a bench, or sitting on the grass, or walking by him at that very moment. Kids were so damn desperate for something juicy to talk about, something to add to their boring lives and infinitely repeated conversations. The news of Sam's new suspect status must have already spread throughout all of NYU—and probably the rest of the tristate area as well.

"Forget him, Sam," Josh said, flicking Sam's head with a lighthearted slap. "Any friend who could turn on you so fast is no friend, dude. That kid's an asshole."

San tried to smile, but his lips felt like sandpaper. This was no good. He couldn't take his eyes off Brendan's retreating form "I really thought he was . . . I don't know. He didn't used to be—"

"Forget it, Sam, come on," Josh said. "It's your move. Let's play, poodle boy. Tell me more about Gaia."

Sam turned back to the board. He wanted to keep playing, to talk more about Gaia, to do anything to take his mind off Mike Suarez . . . but he couldn't. Still, at least he had Josh. The guy didn't act at all like an RA. He acted like a friend. Judging from the way everyone had been looking at Sam lately, Josh was fast turning into the only friend he had. And Josh hardly even *knew* him.

"Thank you, man," Sam found himself blurting out.

Josh grinned, cocking his eyebrow. "For what?"

"For everything. For hanging out, and for listening to me babble about Gaia, and for not believing the crap those cops were saying about me."

"You don't have to thank me," Josh replied with a shrug. "I've seen some messed-up shit and some messed-up people, and I know a good guy when I see one. I'm just chilling, Sam." He smirked. "Besides, it's my university-bound duty to help the students I advise to cope with their problems—"

"Well, hel-*lo*, Mr. Moon and Tom Cruise!"

Sam whirled to his left. His heart snapped back into overdrive. Detectives Bernard and Reilly were approaching the table, wrapped up in cheap trench coats, smiling as if they'd just won the lottery. Sam didn't get it. They were relentless. They were everywhere he was—all the time.

"I am so very glad to see you two again," Bernard called. He turned to his partner. "Look, Reilly, it's just two college chums having a rousing game of chess. Isn't that special? Ah, the life of privilege. What a shame when it all goes to waste."

"Well, hello, officers!" Josh answered, matching every ounce of Bernard's sarcasm. "Our chess game has been delightful. As has our life of privilege! Thank you for the ignorant stereotyping. Saaay, how are your doughnuts?"

Sam cringed. Maybe that was just a little too over the top. . . .

"I'll handle this," Bernard insisted, trying to shut up his partner. "We just stopped by to commend your dormitory security guard for being so kind and cooperative." Bernard pulled a piece of paper out of his pocket, unfolded it, and snapped it in front of Sam and Josh's faces. "Once I showed him our *search warrant*, he was nothing but a joy. So I guess we'll be in touch shortly? Have a nice day."

ONE THING GAIA'S LIFE HAD DEFI-

nitely lacked in the past few days was stillness. But sitting Indian style on her hotel bed, wearing her wrinkled flannel shirt and her pajama bottoms at 3:00 A.M., she had finally found herself a silent moment. Her father was fast asleep in the bed across the room. She was glad. She needed a moment to herself, just to think. Without any distractions.

Un-Gaia-like Wild Puppies

The room was soothing in its spare beauty. An oak table covered one wall almost entirely. Her father and she had each taken one of the two spacious beds with white silk sheets and majestic oak headboards. The wall to her right had a pair of tall French doors, covered by long, flowing white drapes, that led onto a small, graceful, wrought-iron terrace. And on the table and by each bed were these perfect little baroque lamps that cast only as much light as was necessary.

Sitting in silence, hearing only the ticking of the wooden clock on the wall, with only one shaft of warm lamplight, Gaia watched her father sleep. She knew she wouldn't be able to sleep herself—and it had nothing to do with jet lag. Her eyes fell to the crusty bruise on his temple. Hard to believe that only four days ago, she'd assaulted him. Of course, she'd believed with all her heart that he was . . . someone else. Her uncle. That sick—

Ella. It all came back to Ella—to that conversation they'd had in that Alphabet City hellhole. The whole time Ella had talked about Loki, she'd actually been talking about Oliver, not her father. Suddenly Gaia flashed back to all those "sweet" moments with Oliver: every one of them a manipulation, a plot, a scheme. His "cancer" was probably just another lie concocted to reel her in, too. Saving her life in the park that night still didn't quite fit in, but Gaia couldn't figure it all out now. . . .

There was no point driving herself crazy, though. Ella was dead. Loki was incarcerated (for now, anyway). She had her dad. She had Sam—

Sam.

The name was like an oversized bite of ice cream: so sweet, but so painful. It sent a shiver of regret through her heart. But she knew—now more than ever—that she'd made the right decision to leave him. It was only temporary. Still, she couldn't remember ever feeling such longing as she did at this very moment. It was so strange. Every emotion she usually kept at arm's length, or veiled in humor, had suddenly broken through, left to gambol around her mind like a new litter of wild puppies. She couldn't control them. Then again, she didn't necessarily want to control them. . . .

Tell Sam. Tell him right now. You'll probably be you again by morning. Don't let this moment go to waste.

And then it hit her: She would write a love letter.

Yes. She would do something so totally un-Gaia-like, so totally the opposite of everything she'd stood for during the past five years, that it would be this magical, transformative experience. Given the precariousness and fragility of her life right now, she knew there was a very good chance she might not have this opportunity again. The moment was like a slippery ball of glass. She couldn't hold on to it forever. Soon it would drop and shatter. She had to act.

94

Without another moment's hesitation Gaia jumped from her bed and tiptoed over to her father's laptop on the oak table. Looking back at her sleeping father, she grabbed the laptop and tiptoed into the coat closet, making sure the phone cord didn't come unplugged. She closed the door, carefully slipping the phone cord underneath it, then pulled the chain to flip on the one stark lightbulb on the ceiling. Then she sat down, flipped open the computer, and logged on to her e-mail.

Dearest Sam, she typed.

Ugh, too cheesy. She pounded on the delete button until the screen was blank again.

Dear Sam, she typed.

But that was just a letter. Not a love letter. She attacked the delete button once again.

Sam, she typed.

Sam? "Sam, don't forget to pick up cat food." "Sam, please drop off the dry cleaning." That's how a person addressed a goddamn refrigerator note....

Gai scowled. *And now the moment's gone,* she thought with a flash of her usual cynicism. *I never should have tried to write this stuff down. Now I'm totally self-conscious....*

No. Gaia wasn't ready to let it go. Not yet. She was the new Gaia. The new Gaia who could smile ... the one with her family just on the other side of the door.

The new Gaia in love.

From: gaia13@alloymail.com
To: smoon@alloymail.com
Re: You
Time: 3:21 A.M.

Dear Sam,

I wish I could have told you how I was feeling about four minutes ago because four minutes ago, I knew exactly what I wanted to say. But once I decided to write it down, I seemed to have no idea how to say it. Does that make sense? Well, that's what happened.

I'm not a quitter, though. That's something you should know about me by now, so here I am, still not knowing how to say it but writing anyway because I've told myself that I'm not allowed to stop writing even though I don't know how to say it and with each word I'm sounding more and more like an *idiot*, which is exactly what I was afraid of.

But I'm not stopping.

So I'm just going to tell you what I'm feeling. Hopefully, when I'm done, I'll have a love letter.

That's what this is supposed to be, by the way. A love letter. It's pretty shitty so far, huh? I just don't really do "happy" so well. I think of myself as a fairly articulate person, but reading what I have just written . . . well, let's just say it isn't college essay material.

It's just that I haven't been happy in so long
that my synapses don't really know how to cope.
My life has taken this crazy turn and I've got
you and I've got my father back and I think I
must have been magically beamed into someone
else's life, except it's my life. It's mine.

You're mine.

Forget the college essay. This is starting to
sound like a really, really lame-ass Hallmark card.
But I'm not stopping. There's so much you don't even
know. I can't possibly explain it all now, but I
didn't go to Germany with my uncle. I went to Paris
with my father. Long story. I'll tell you in person.

For the time being, let me try to make an anal-
ogy to help you understand what my life has become.

My dad and I were at Notre Dame Cathedral. Right
in front of the main facade of the cathedral, there's
a gold sort of compass star set in the pavement, not
really even that big. It says, "Point Zero." It's the
center of all of Paris. The entire city is measured
from that one golden star. And that's what my life
feels like. I feel like, from now on, everything that
happens in my life should really start with this
point. This is my point zero. I'm starting my life
from this point in this hotel with my father. I'm
starting from this point with *you*, Sam.

That's what I'm trying to say.

Before I met you, I'd never in my life

experienced that feeling that I just had four minutes ago, now I guess five or six minutes ago. The feeling that made me have to write this letter. In a way it was kind of like being sick.

You know how they say there's a fine line between pleasure and pain? You know, like the way laughing can suddenly turn into crying or the other way around? Well, I was lying in my bed here in the hotel, and when I thought of you, I felt like—sort of like I was sick but without any of the pain of sickness. I was sort of shivering.

Never mind.

By the way, if you ever show this to another living soul, I will *kill you*. And I mean that. I actually can and actually will kill you.

I love you, Sam. I love you so much, it kind of hurts. And I miss you.

Okay. I think this was sort of a love letter. It's a good start, anyway. But you know, this is just point zero. I'm just getting started here. I promise these letters will get better. But it's not a real love letter until I press send, so I'm going to press send now.

Have I got balls or what?

I love you,

Gaia

P.S. I wonder if you're thinking about me right now.

The thing that seems so strange to me now is that I was so sure I was in love with Sam Moon. I mean, Sam was the perfect guy. He was intelligent, he was in college, he was hot. (Still is, actually.) I would have done anything for Sam when we were going out. I would have done whatever he wanted, wherever he wanted. I couldn't even picture my life without him.

But it turns out . . . .

That was nothing. That wasn't love.

In the last few days I've remembered what true love is. I remember what it feels like. I remember how it kills brain cells so you end up washing your face with the shampoo and trying to shave your legs with the toothbrush. I remember what it's like to forget where you're going between the kitchen and the dining room or not to realize people are talking to you—so that by the time you realize, you have no idea what they're talking about. You can't concentrate on anything because every single second is spent just thinking of *him*. Just picturing *him*.

I remember it so well because the only two times I've ever felt that way in my life, it's been with the same guy. I just wish we'd never been apart. I let that stupid accident get in the way of that feeling. If we'd just stayed together the whole time, then I could always tell people that it was love at first sight and that we'd been together ever since.

And it was love at first sight. I don't even think I've ever told Ed the truth about how I used to look out the window of the Astor Place Starbucks to watch him skate. How lame is that? I know, but it's true. I used to "conveniently" end up at the corner table by the window with Megan and some of my other friends every day at three. And then, sipping latte and using a

few well-placed "uh-huhs" and
"oh, totallys," I could watch him
for an hour without them ever
even knowing.

I'd scan down from his mussed-
up brown hair, through his confi-
dent devilish smile, to some
long-sleeve T-shirt—it was always
too big, but you could still tell
he had a great body—to the low-
hanging worn-out jeans, down to
his worn-out vintage Puma sneak-
ers. I guess I was a little
obsessed.

Of course, once we found each
other, I think I can safely say
he was, too. We were inseparable.
It was perfect. It was true love,
it was first love, it was my
"first time," it was perfect.

Nothing should have ever torn
us apart.

But that doesn't matter now.
Because we're together again and
that makes me the luckiest girl
in the world. I am with my first
and only true love. And I will
never let him go again. I can't

even believe I'd ever thought for
a second that twenty-six million
dollars had anything to do with
my wanting Ed back. I mean, I was
just as in love with him before
we'd even spoken—back when he was
just a scruffy skate rat who
didn't even know I was watching
him—back when he'd do skateboard
stunts for a dollar just so he
could afford a Rice Krispy treat.
That's the Ed I love. That's the
Ed I will always love. For richer
or poorer. In sickness and in
health. For as long as we both
shall live.

Okay. I'll calm down. I guess
I'm a little young to get married.

But in a few years . . .

Hmmm. *Heather Fargo*. It does
have a kind of downtown super-
model ring to it. . . .

Something about Heather's tone had just . . . besides being thrown him disturbing a little. It was so mercenary.

"AH, MONSIEUR FARGO, *BON SOIR*. Ze lady, she has already arrived. Follow me, please."

X-Rated Body

French. Of course Heather had chosen a French restaurant. Capsouto Frères. Heather said that it was "not necessarily all that trendy" (a classic Heather-style understatement) and "only mildly overpriced" (ditto), but very romantic.

That last part Ed didn't mind at all. And looking around, he saw that the place was actually very cool—a lot of space, with pristine blond wooden floors and big windows covered with long, flowing white drapes. There were lots of candles, too, reflecting off the shiny copper work on the ceiling in a warm, golden glow.

Now Ed felt it was worth it to have put on his black suit. He wasn't a suit kind of guy, but it fit the occasion. He just prayed that he wouldn't have to eat any frogs' legs or snails. There was absolutely nothing romantic about that. He could not understand how anyone in their right mind would want to eat a snail.

"Euh, eef you don't mind me saying, monsieur," the maitre d' muttered from the side of his mouth, looking down at Ed as they wove through the maze of beautiful people, "your sister, she is *très belle, monsieur*, very beautiful."

Sister. Ed smirked. Of course. How could a guy in a wheelchair have a girl like that, right?

Ed was very used to that kind of moronic short-sightedness. He actually managed to get a kick out of it a lot of the time. People were funny in their ignorance. But tonight was just one of those nights; for some reason, it pissed him off. He considered running over the chubby waiter's foot. But Ed didn't want to risk getting kicked out. Besides, there might just be a day, not so far in the future, when Ed wouldn't have to put up with this kind of crap anymore.

Correction. There wasn't any "might" about it. That day would come.

Ed had been working his butt off the past few days in physical therapy. He'd actually had to blow Heather off a few times because he wasn't ready to come back to school yet. He'd told her that he'd caught a mean case of the flu at his aunt's house. Heather didn't even seem to mind that she wasn't allowed to come see him. She didn't seem to mind anything these days. It was as if Ed could do no wrong.

And this would be the first time they'd seen each other since his return. Face-to-face. He was brimming with so many different crazy emotions, it was getting harder and harder to keep his cool. His palms moistened as he maneuvered his way through the restaurant. This was the night. The night Ed was going to tell Heather about the amazing news.

She'd be ready for it, too. Her e-mail had said everything he needed to hear. Ed opened it at least three times a day. Every day. He especially liked to read it during that hormonal high that always followed a grueling physical therapy session. He couldn't get over it.

His life was changing so fast, it was almost as if too many good things were happening at the same time. To have his legs back *and* have Heather back the way he'd had her before? It would be like picking up right where Shred left off, when his life was at its most perfect—like wiping the accident and the horrible breakup right off the record—like going back in time. Who wouldn't go back in time if they had the chance just to fix things?

Ed forgot the answer to that question. He forgot the question. He forgot his own name when the sight of Heather Gannis entered his eyes and swept through his body like a neon blue electric current.

Heather stood up from the table.

Ed's eyes traveled down her ivory-sculpted neck and shoulders, past that long dark hair to her short, black dress. The hem barely cleared her knees. What Ed could not believe was that he'd forgotten that Heather's actual body was so much more perfect than the body he'd *imagined* in all his X-rated fantasies of the last week. Maybe because it was so much more elegant than an X-rated body. It was . . . well, it was Heather's body.

The next thing he knew, her legs had straddled his lap, her hands had clamped onto the back of his chair, and her lips were on his in a deep, wet, powerful kiss. Ed succumbed completely. He shut his eyes as his hands grabbed onto the back of her head, and for a brief moment there was no sound but their own breathing. Finally Heather slid off his lap.

"Hi," she said with sweet simplicity, and then sat back down.

Ed blinked. He could hardly breathe. He certainly couldn't move. Everyone around them stared at their plates.

The maitre d' looked horrified.

Ed smiled up at him. "God, I've missed my sister," he said.

"Yes, monsieur." The man scowled, then scampered off.

After a few deep breaths Ed managed to gather himself enough to pull up across the table from Heather.

"Sister?" Heather asked, frowning as she took a sip of water.

"Not important," Ed mumbled with a grin. His eyes roved over her again. "You look . . . unbelievable."

"You too," Heather replied.

Ed could feel his face getting hot. "Um—Um . . . ," he stammered. "Thank you for that . . . kiss."

"Oh, don't thank me now," Heather whispered as

the waiter handed them their menus. "Thank me later."

"Shut up," Ed murmured. He couldn't wipe the idiotic smile off his face. "I won't be able to eat if you keep acting like this."

"So sue me."

He glanced at her again. Heather had become much more emotional in this new incarnation of their relationship, much more open about her needs than she had been in the old days of Heather and Shred. She'd always prided herself on her poise in any situation. She used to talk about how her mother had taught her "grace under pressure" and how to "keep them guessing."

But tonight Heather seemed so desperately emotional, it was almost out of character. And Ed liked it. Every sexual impulse was showing—every ounce of her joy—how much she seemed to need him and, most of all, how much she loved him. When she heard the news, she was going to flip.

"Do you want me to tell you the news now, or should we wait?" Ed asked, placing his hands over Heather's.

"Tell me now."

Ed nodded. He took her hands into his own and thought: *Take your time.* But it was no use. He couldn't contain himself. In a mad rush the news tumbled from Ed's mouth: the surgery, the white lie about his aunt's house, Dr. Feldman, the mixed feelings of fear and ambivalence and excitement, the freezing cold recovery, that indescribable moment when Dr. Feldman told him that the surgery was a success . . . Brian, his WWF rock-obsessed lunatic physical therapist, the grueling workouts for hours a day, and wanting to kill Brian for the pain he was inflicting and then wanting to hug him whenever it was over. . . .

Heather just kept shaking her head. Her blue eyes widened, searching his face. Her lips quivered. One moment it looked like she might burst out laughing; the next, it looked like she would break down in tears.

Finally Ed took a deep breath. There was still one thing he couldn't bring himself to mention . . . in some ways, the hardest thing of all. It was his confusion—confusion over the chair itself.

After two years he'd not only gotten used to being in the chair, he'd come to accept it. And then there were his feelings of guilt and hypocrisy for potentially leaving behind all the other handicapped folks who didn't have a choice. In a way, wouldn't he be some kind of sellout—claiming that the quality of life didn't have to be any worse in a chair but then dying to get out of it? He saw the situation kind of like when a big rap star shoots to the top, rapping about the 'hood and demanding respect for all the brothers and sisters in the 'hood. Then he makes a fat wad of cash, and two seconds later he drops the 'hood for a phat pad in Beverly Hills right next to Kenny G. Ed didn't want to feel like he was betraying his chair-bound brothers and sisters . . .

But the excitement was too much to handle.

"This morning," he said, leaning closer to Heather's beautiful face. "I moved my left pinkie toe. I swear, I told my foot to move, and my toe actually heard me. Do you know what that means? That means it's working, Heather. I am—"

Before Ed knew what was happening, Heather had jumped out of her seat and into Ed's lap, kissing him and hugging him and kissing him again, tears pouring down her face. Ed couldn't believe it. This was like a scene from a movie: It was the exact response he'd dreamed of every night since the surgery. Pure unadulterated joy.

"I am so happy for you," she sobbed. "You deserve it, Ed. You deserve it. You deserve everything."

They kissed again.

Finally Heather pulled herself away from Ed and slumped back into her seat, wiping the tears from her eyes. "God," she murmured, looking almost embarrassed. "I thought you were going to tell me something completely different."

Ed laughed. "What?"

Heather just shook her head and sniffled.

"Nothing. I thought it was going to be good news about your settlement, that's all."

"Oh, the settlement." Ed sighed. Funny. He hadn't even thought of that. Not once in over two weeks. "Yeah, well, we can kiss that good-bye." He picked up the menu, scanning it for terms like *cheeseburger* among the endless list of alien French phrases.

"What do you mean . . . kiss it good-bye?" Heather asked.

"Well, you know," he said. "I mean, if it turns out the damage wasn't irreparable, that's going to be a whole other story. They'll probably get most of the money back in the appeal. Which is fine. I mean, I never wanted their money."

"But you said . . ." Heather's voice tapered off, and then it stopped altogether.

Ed glanced up.

Heather was crying again. Only . . . these didn't look like the same tears of joy from a few moments ago. No. Something had changed. She kept her eyes focused to the side, away from Ed, almost as if she didn't want him to look at her. Whatever thin piece of emotional elastic had held her together snapped as she dropped her head in her hands and hid her face from Ed.

"Oh God, I'm sorry," she cried quietly. Her mascara was starting to run. "I'm so sorry, Ed. I don't want to ruin this night for you. I . . . I'm just going to run to the bathroom and wash up for a second." Without another word, she snatched up her purse and bolted from the table.

Ed's jaw dropped. He felt like a knife had been plunged into his heart. What on earth was she so upset about all of a sudden? He pulled out from behind the table and moved closer to her chair, to comfort her when she came back. For a few seconds he felt ill—ashamed. He'd been so wrapped up in himself and his own issues that he hadn't even asked or cared what was going on with her. . . .

A minute later she returned. She seemed to have calmed down a bit; her makeup had been fixed, and she was no longer crying. She eased herself into her chair and forced a brittle smile.

"What is it, Heather?" he whispered. "What's wrong?"

"Well . . . my life is a complete wreck," she admitted. Her shoulders sagged, as if she'd given up. Her smile rapidly faded. "Phoebe's a stick, and my parents can't afford her recovery anymore. And they're fighting about money all the time, and my dad can't find a job, and I'm afraid they're gonna split up, Ed, I really am, and I'm hiding from my friends 'cause I can't afford to hang out with them anymore. All this money stuff—"

"It's okay," Ed assured her, stroking her hair. "It's okay. Calm down."

"I just thought . . ." she mumbled as she tried to

catch her breath. "I just thought that you'd be able to help me, Ed—to help us, my whole family. Like you said . . . you know, before all *this* . . ."

Another dagger stabbed through Ed's chest. Shame and guilt washed over him like a flash flood. "I would have," he insisted. "If I had that money, I'd do anything I could to help."

"I *know*." Heather moaned. "I know you would, Ed. You've always kept your promises. It's just . . . that money was going to fix everything. Without that money, I don't know what I'm going to do. What am I going to do?"

"I—I . . . don't know," Ed stammered, lightly kissing Heather's forehead. "I mean . . . I know how these cases go down . . . if I walk again, then the liability is totally different. That's just the way things work. . . . I'm so sorry. . . ."

Ed realized that he was now apologizing for the possibility that he might walk again. It was an extraordinarily disconcerting feeling—even on top of everything else. But just when he thought he'd have to remove Heather from the restaurant on a stretcher with the help of an oxygen tank, she stopped crying. She pulled her head up to Ed with a bright glimmer in her eye.

"But what if . . ." she uttered. "No, forget it; that's so stupid." She shook her head angrily and snatched up her menu, her brow tightly furrowed.

"No, what?" Ed encouraged her. "What is it?"

Heather lifted her head again and probed Ed's eyes before she spoke.

"Well . . . what if they didn't know you could walk?"

ED'S HAND WENT LIMP ON HEATHER'S
shoulder, and then it fell away.

"What are you talking about?" he asked.

Heather couldn't help but detect a fraction of the sweetness dropping from his voice, replaced by some combination of confu-

The One Thing

sion . . . and something else. Her heart squeezed. That something else had the potential to turn into anger. She knew it. She should have kept her mouth shut. *No, no, no*—she was just so desperate . . . and this would work. Yes. She just prayed Ed wouldn't turn on her, not now, because she had it all figured out.

It had come to her in a rush. The perfect solution to everybody's problems: a simple little white lie. Besides, he'd lied to her, right? About his aunt's house. About being sick. This was really no worse. . . .

"Okay, wait," Heather said, taking Ed's hand and squeezing it for dear life. "Please just hear me out for a second, Ed." She wiped away her remaining tears. "There is something you could do, and it wouldn't even be that hard, and it wouldn't even take that long."

The look in Ed's eyes softened. "Okay," he said, squeezing her hand back.

"Okay," Heather echoed happily. "Aren't you pretty close to getting that money?"

Ed narrowed his gaze slightly as if to say, *Where exactly are you going with this?* "Yeah," he finally replied with a slight shrug. "I mean, I won the case. It's just in appeal."

"And there's no way they'd win the appeal, right?" Heather asserted.

"Well, I'm saying," Ed explained, "if I walk again—"

"Right, but if you couldn't walk again . . ." Heather interrupted. She was maintaining eye contact obsessively. Looking in Ed's eyes, she could read his shifting emotions. And right now, he was starting to doubt her; she could see it. He was an open-minded guy, but this might be a little much—

"I don't know what you're talking about," Ed murmured with a tense shrug. "Why don't you just tell me what you're talking about?"

"Okay," she said, rubbing her hand along his arm—struggling with every ounce of her strength and will to appear both relaxed and seductive. "Here's what I'm saying: If you just . . . pretended for a little while that you weren't making progress . . . I mean until you got the settlement, then . . . you'd get everything."

There was a long, dead silence.

Ed's expressionless face just hung there—as if someone had pressed the pause button. All at once she felt sick. What was she doing? The thought of what might or might not be running through his mind at this moment was unbearable. It ate away at the lining of her stomach like a cramp. . . .

If Heather had learned anything in her experience with boys so far, it was this: It only took one thing. At any given moment, no matter how long two people went out, you might say that *one thing* that would totally change the other person's mind, make them reassess you and leave you in the dust. Of course, she'd never really cared too much about saying that one thing with anyone but Ed. And now she was terrified that she'd just said it. Ed probably thought she was a horrible person for even conceiving of it. He probably thought that she was some conniving moneygrubbing bitch. But he was wrong. He was so wrong. She just had to prove it.

"Pretend I can't do the one thing I've wanted to do for years?" Ed asked. He shot Heather a piercing, incredulous glance. "So I can scam the New York court system? That's your suggestion?"

116

"Shhh." Heather raised her hand over Ed's mouth. "God," she whispered. "Don't look at it like that."

He laughed, but he was frowning. "Well, how should I look at it? I mean, you're joking, right? You can't be serious."

Hopelessness began to well up inside her once more. She could hear the doubt in his voice, the fear. It had been a perfect evening just minutes ago—and now he was glaring at her like she was some petty little schemer. Couldn't he see the immensity of the situation?

"Ed," she said. "You just said to me that if there was anything you could do, you'd do it."

"I know, but—"

"Don't you understand? There is something you can do." Heather drew in her breath and forced a smile. "Besides, when did you turn into the world's most upstanding citizen?" She was trying to joke with him, but her words ended up sounding stiff, tense. "When did you start caring about the New York court system, for God's sake? Don't you remember how you used to feel about the cops when they'd mess with you just because you had scruffy hair and a skateboard?"

"Well, yeah," Ed admitted with a fleeting smile.

Good. A smile is good. Now just be honest with him.

"Ed," Heather said gently, taking both of his hands. "You have the power to help my whole family. And besides, you *deserve* that money after what you've been

117

through, whether you ever walk again or not. And who in their right mind just waves bye-bye to a totally deserved twenty-six million dollars?"

Ed shook his head, but now he was laughing. He bit his lip and looked very seriously into Heather's eyes. Heather looked back with all the love that was in her heart. Maybe, just maybe, she was beginning to make sense to him.

I CAN'T BELIEVE I'M ACTUALLY EVEN
considering this.

Ed stared into Heather's eyes. Those beautiful, wicked, anguished, sexy blue eyes. The eyes that had brought him so much joy and so much misery. The eyes that wiped the past clean. The eyes that promised a future of happiness.

Too Much Chair Jumping

And she had a point. All he'd have to do was delay his recovery just a few weeks while they worked on securing that settlement. And in doing so, he'd be saving not only the woman he loved, but the entire family of the woman he loved. He'd be doing something good. Something positive.

Besides, the family who had done this to him *did* deserve to pay for the damage they had wrought. Didn't they?

Deep down, he loved that Heather trusted him enough to expose such weakness to him. It proved that their relationship was stronger than ever. And he loved that he had something that could give her back her strength and bring her such instant happiness. But mostly Ed loved that he had the chance to be a hero. And how often did a guy really have the chance to be someone else's hero? Especially a guy in a wheelchair? Certain friends of Ed's could never see him as the hero—certain blond, beautiful, badass friends (who would remain nameless) were such heroes in their own right that they never gave Ed the *chance* to be truly heroic.

But not Heather. She needed him. He was her savior. He placed his hands on Heather's face and drew her to him. He brought his lips to hers. Heather dropped her shoulders and leaned back her head, surrendering to him.

Finally he pulled away.

"I'll do it," he said.

Heather leaped up and threw her arms around him. He could feel her chest heaving. He could feel her wet tears against his cheek.

"Thank you," she whispered. "I love you, Ed."

"I love you, too," he said, his nose and lips nestled in her silky hair. As gently as he could, he maneuvered her back into her seat. Suddenly he realized he was exhausted. There had been far too much drama tonight, far too much chair jumping. It was time to chill.

"Hey—are you hungry?" he asked.

She giggled. "Starving."

He breathed a sigh of relief and picked up the menu for the third time. Well. Now they could actually settle down and—

"So you can't tell anyone, Ed," Heather stated.

Ed looked up. "Huh?"

"No matter how much feeling you might—I mean you do—gain in your legs, you can't tell a soul. You and I are the only ones who can know about it."

"Uh—uh . . . well," he stammered, not sure what to make of this. Couldn't they just eat first before they got into any specifics?

"Ed, I'm totally serious," Heather muttered, glancing around the restaurant. "You can't tell anyone. Not your doctor, not your parents, not even your physical therapist. Not until that settlement is final."

Ed blinked. Wow. Something about Heather's tone had just . . . thrown him a little. It was so mercenary. Which in a weird way—besides being disturbing—was kind of sexy, too. He patted her shoulder. Heather's brow relaxed, and her face brightened.

"Don't worry," he said. "You're gonna be fine."

SAM'S DORM ROOM LOOKED LIKE IT

Rubble had been hit by a tornado—and pretty much any other natural disaster one could think of. Literally. He was used to a mess . . . but this was sheer destruction. They'd rummaged through every single piece of clothing, every CD case, every book, every notebook, every goddamn tube of toothpaste. And they hadn't cleaned up a thing.

They'd taken his insulin kit. They'd even taken his computer.

He went numb. He could only stand there and survey the wreckage. His anger fell away. His despair fell away. Maybe this was how shock actually felt. He wasn't sure. He wasn't even asking himself the same old questions he'd been asking for weeks. Why me? What have I done to deserve this? When will I be free from all this? He was just a body. Just another object amidst the rubble.

I'm dead, he thought coldly. *This is purgatory. And I am dead.*

"I'm sorry, Sam," Josh said behind him. "I really am."

Ted Koehler from down the hall ducked his head into Sam's room. Without knocking. He and Sam had maybe exchanged five words in their entire lives. And from the prying look on Ted's face, he was just another sniveling, suspicious gossip hound sniffing around Sam's life. Sam couldn't take another minute of it. Without thinking, he picked up the biggest book within his immediate reach and hurled it at the wall.

"Get the hell out!" Sam screamed as the book smashed against the plaster—leaving a huge black mark.

Ted Koehler bolted.

And then Sam was numb again.

WHAT A BIZARRE EVENING, ED

thought as he rolled along Charles Street, the icy wind beating hard against his face.

Heather had wanted to see him all the way home, but Ed had decided that tonight wasn't such a good night for it. He needed to think. Besides, they'd taken a nice long walk after dinner—strolling through their favorite parts of the Village, even revisiting some of their secret make-out spots from back in the day. There was an excellent secluded park bench down by the Horatio Street basketball courts where they used to go all the time. No one ever walked by there after ten. So they'd hung out there for a while and kissed, then they moved on. They'd found nooks and crannies every few blocks where they'd share some kisses before moving on again. But after a while Ed had simply tired. He'd called it a night and sent Heather home in a cab.

It wasn't just the confusion, the apprehension. It was everything. He was totally wrung out from the emotional Tilt-A-Whirl of the dinner, and he was also physically beat from the therapy. He couldn't believe that this was his first night out since he'd been discharged from the hospital. He'd packed about as much into it as he had in the last two years put together. Well, except for the nights he'd been with Gaia—those wild nights around Thanksgiving time with Mary...

He shook his head. Thinking of Gaia reminded him of school. And tomorrow would be his first day back. Shit. He'd need all of his energy. The thought of Brian working him over in the evenings after The Village School worked him over during the days ... Jesus. That was enough to wreak serious havoc on his body and his mind—not counting the addition of the lies that would be required to convince everyone that he wasn't making any progress.

He shook his head, shivering as he rolled along the sidewalk. The weird thing was, the more momentum he picked up, the less tired he felt. It was as if his exhaustion had carried into some weird state beyond exhaustion. His bones ached; he could barely think; but for some reason, he was wide awake. He didn't know what he was feeling: It was something he couldn't put his finger on. It was a kind of . . . well, a sort of gross sensation in the pit of his stomach, coupled with an annoying pressure on his temples.

Sleep, he said to himself. Right. He just needed to get home and get some sleep.

Only . . .

Ed began to notice that he wasn't actually going in the direction of his home. As if acting of their own free will, his hands seemed to have wheeled him on a detour farther into the West Village. And with his mind racing, he hadn't quite noticed that he'd made a turn off Charles Street onto Perry Street. Next thing he knew, he was just a few doors down from Gaia's house.

Maybe she was home.

The windows were dark, but that meant nothing.

She might still be there.

He rolled to a stop in front of the wheelchair-friendly entrance—one of the few in the city, at least as far as brownstones were concerned. Not that he would be needing it anymore. Not after the settlement . . .

Why hadn't she called him when he'd been out of school so long? Were things still awkward between them? He could just ring her doorbell right now and get all this bullshit out in the open. There was no reason for things to be strained between them just because Ed was seeing Heather again. So what if Gaia and Heather despised each other with a passion? Those two really needed to just throw on some gloves and go a few rounds in the ring. Settle their differences—

What am I saying? That would be like Jean-Claude Van Damme against some little . . . I don't know, like that little mini–Backstreet Boy Aaron Carter kid. Although actually, I wouldn't mind seeing that kid get a little Van Dammed . . .

He stared at the door. He could just go up for a few minutes. Tell her about—

Ed stopped himself midthought. Of course he couldn't. He couldn't tell her about his surgery. He couldn't tell *anyone* about it. Without really thinking, he rolled up the ramp. He looked through the front door window, but it was pitch black. All he could see was the circle of frost from his own breath on the glass of the door. He pulled back a foot and looked up at Gaia's floor. Pitch black. From here, so close, the entire town house looked . . . dead. Vacant. Not just like no one was living there. Like no one ever *had* lived there.

Ed took a long, deep breath and blew it out as he slumped down in his chair. He moved his face an inch from the glass one more time to peer inside, for no good reason. There was nothing to see but another circle of icy white formed by his breath. Finally Ed raised his finger and wrote a four-letter word in the frost.

Gaia.

He only wanted to talk to her for a few minutes. He *needed* to talk to her. It had been too long. And that's when he realized what the feeling was that he couldn't quite put his finger on.

He was depressed.

So. I told Heather my news at the restaurant, and her reaction was *perfect*. It was exactly what I wanted it to be. She was thrilled. She was just as ecstatic as I was. It was like she could see the whole future for us that I'd been seeing. The one with all those possibilities.

But I don't know how long it was, three minutes? Four minutes later? And we were talking about *money*. It was just . . . weird.

Money is weird. I mean, who really cares about money? Obviously Heather does. In a way, it defines her friends' social status. Not that she's as shallow as her friends . . . but still. And her family cares about money for sure. I guess everybody does. I don't know. I guess I'm the weird one for not caring.

But from the second we started talking about my settlement, the same damn thought kept popping into my head like a jack-in-the-box. I had to keep cramming it

back under its lid. I just couldn't
help wondering: If I'd told Gaia
my news, how would she have
responded? Would the word *money*
ever have fallen from her lips in
that conversation?

I doubt it. She knows what
it's like to be robbed of something more important than money.
Just like I do. She's been robbed
of a family, a home. I've been
robbed of my legs. Compared to
that, money really seems kind of
silly.

Then again, maybe we're just
both weird.

Sometimes being disabled had perverse advantages.

real anger

SAM COULDN'T SEE ANY POINT TO

getting out of bed. He'd let his
clock-radio alarm play on for five
minutes before it finally turned
itself off. It was one of those
"wacky" morning talk shows with
lots of sound effects, some "dumb
Italian" character, Eddie Spaghetti

Back to Sleep

or something—and the requisite "slick-talking" guy
who makes inane jokes while some poor woman is
forced to laugh at them.

In other words, it was the perfect
bonus to go with the tortured purgatory
he reluctantly called his life.

After the radio went off, he tried to go back to
sleep. He could sleep for days. What was the point
of going outside? So he could endure more petty
frightened stares and cold shoulders from his ignorant classmates? Why go to class? To study up for
his defense when they hauled him off to jail? Too
bad he was premed. He really should have been
prelaw. . . .

*Jail. I wonder what it's going to be like in jail. I won-
der if it's anything like Oz—that show I saw on HBO
when I went home for Christmas—with crazed white
supremacists and rapists and killers and—*

Sam turned over in his bed. He pulled his pasty
eyelids apart to see the time. Once his vision finally

focused, he could see it was 11:12 A.M. He still wasn't ready to get up, though. Not by a long shot.

What do they even have on me?

Whenever he asked himself that question—which was pretty much every few minutes—that's when the real anger kicked in. He looked around at the nuclear aftermath that was his room. He hadn't even bothered to clean it up. There was no point. No doubt they'd be back again. Bernard and Reilly were certainly tenacious; he had to give them credit for that. But he couldn't help but wonder . . .what made them so sure he was guilty? A lifelong diabetic's insulin kit? A couple of undeleted e-mails from Ella on his computer? They probably thought he killed Mike over some woman. As if Sam would ever have done something like that for Ella Niven—

At the mere thought of Ella, Sam's rage got the better of him. He threw the covers off his body and hurled them into the wreckage. The sight of his own pale, thin body made him ill. He was losing it—his health, his sanity, everything. He truly wished Ella were still alive. That way, he could kill her himself. Every ounce of this tragedy was her doing. If he could just tell someone about her . . .

That was the horrible irony of this whole situation. This entire investigation was intended to uncover who killed Mike Suarez. And Sam already *knew* who killed Mike. But who was going to believe him? Nothing like a mysterious dead woman to bolster your case. Ella might as well have been the "one-armed man." Or why not Dracula? Or the werewolf? The cops would believe any of those stories just as easily.

I could tell Josh about her, Sam thought, almost desperately. *At least then someone else would know the truth.*

But if he told Josh, Sam would probably lose the one guy he could even come *close* to calling a friend. No doubt such a crazy story would only frighten Josh away. And Sam didn't think he could deal with that. Still, what if the cops started asking about Ella? Someone other than Sam needed to know the truth if it ever came down to a trial with witnesses and a jury.

Of course, someone else did know the truth. But where was she?

Where are you, Gaia? Don't they have phones in Germany? Why haven't you called me?

He finally won Gaia's heart. They were finally together, and now, when he needed her more than ever, she'd vanished into thin air, somewhere in Germany with her uncle.

All he wanted was to talk to her. Just to talk. Even if only for a few minutes. Everything would feel so much more bearable.

But no. No such luck for the cursed Sam Moon. Which meant only one thing. Back to sleep.

ED KNEW THERE WAS A GOOD CHANCE

The Royal "We"

he might knock a few students down in the hall at this speed. But quite honestly, he didn't care. He had to find out what the hell was going on. *Now.* Besides, it wasn't as if he'd lose any friends by barreling into some meathead jock or pitying girl . . . the kind of girl who avoided looking at him at all costs for fear of acknowledging his wheelchair. He picked up the pace, zooming past lockers and faces and black clothes in a blur, until he reached the office.

People in the office would have the scoop. They seemed to get off on knowing every student's deepest secrets—but never sharing them.

He threw the enforced-glass door wide open and rolled in—then hesitated. He didn't want to come off as too angry, too rude. No. Sometimes being disabled had perverse advantages. He would play up the hurt-puppy-dog angle. He hated to do it—but in this kind of situation, one in which he was asking for a favor . . . well, sometimes it was just best to pander to pity.

"Hi," he said with a smile. "I was wondering—do you know where Gaia Moore is?"

The oldest of them, Mrs. Cross, shook her head. "Can't tell you," she replied brusquely.

"Of course not," he said. His smile faltered. "Did she call in sick or something?"

Mrs. Cross took her glasses (which had been safely nestled in her white hair helmet like another set of eyes) and lifted them down onto her minuscule nose, checking down the list of sick students one by one with her pencil.

"No," she said finally. "Ms. Moore was not sick today. Is that all we want to know?"

Ed shook his head. Amazingly, he was too distraught to be annoyed by the royal "we." He couldn't understand it. He'd checked Gaia's locker between every class. He'd even checked over at Gray's Papaya at lunch. He'd asked around. No one had seen her in a while. *In a while?* It was as if she'd just vanished. Now it was three, and the day was practically over—and Ed was fed up. First the deserted house and now this. He wanted some answers.

"Where is she?" he asked.

"Please, Edward. I thought we—"

"Please *what*? I just want to know where she is. She . . . she's my best friend, all right?"

Mrs. Cross winced. Good. The pity was kicking in.

Another old crone, Mrs. Hadley, shuffled out to the front desk. "Are we having a problem, Mr. Fargo?" she asked.

"Yes, we are having a problem right now," he grumbled, momentarily allowing his frustration to get the best of him. "*We* want to know where Gaia Moore is."

"Well, Mr. Fargo," Mrs. Hadley said. "Ms. Moore is gone."

Ed blinked a few times. The simplicity of her statement sent a sick chill down his back. Her voice was utterly toneless. It was as if she were telling him that the cafeteria was serving meat loaf for lunch or that the school colors had been changed.

"What does that mean?" he asked.

Mrs. Hadley leaned closer to Ed. "It means that Ms. Moore's uncle called the school last week to place Gaia on an indefinite leave of absence. Are we satisfied?"

"No, she wasn't going to—"

Ed stopped himself. There was no point in conversing with this unfortunate but thankfully rare breed of evil elderly people. They didn't need to know what was on his mind—specifically that he knew for a fact that Gaia had decided to stay in the city.

Right. At least . . . that's what she'd told Ed the last time he saw her. Why did she change her mind? When did she change her mind? Why didn't she tell Ed? Yes, he had been away, but how about a simple phone call? She could have e-mailed. She could have at least said good-bye through somebody else. . . .

Without another word, Ed turned around and rolled out of the office. He was numb—absolutely numb. Too numb to be depressed, even. Gaia was gone. For good, probably. Rationally, he knew that he had a better chance of winning the lottery than ever seeing her again. But it just didn't seem possible. No—it couldn't be possible. It was a nightmare, a surreal fantasy gone bad. He wheeled down the hall with his head hanging down over his chest, watching the scuffed linoleum roll under his feet.

The prison cell is no bigger

than a cage. It is filthy, barren. A mattress on the floor. A hole for a toilet. It spits in the face of the Geneva convention. But few international authorities know of this place. It's the kind of prison they reserve for criminals beyond the scope of judicial norms.

I suppose I should feel honored.

They deprive me of nutrition, of human interaction, of any sort of mental or physical stimuli. They mean to break my will. In a way, it's amusing. I never imagined an intelligence agency could be so amateurish. Do they really think they can torture me? Do they think they can prevent me from continuing my work, even as I sit on this fetid mattress? I already have a man on the inside—a man who provides me with all the information I need.

Information about Gaia.

That is the only source of my suffering.

Tom is with her. Now. And
every second he spends with her
adds to the damage I know I will
have to undo.

But I have accepted that. My
private agony only strengthens my
resolve.

And it will make my revenge
all the more sweet.

A flicker of
electricity
shot through
Gaia's body

demolition

as
derby
she took
it. Whatever
this thing
was, it was
heavy.

GAIA'S FATHER HADN'T SAID A WORD

in the past five minutes. All he'd done was gaze at her, with this ethereal, twinkly grin— somewhere between the Cheshire cat and a male version of the *Mona Lisa* (which, ironically, she'd just

I.V. of Attention

seen at the Louvre). Waiters passed. Water and wine were poured. A string trio played Verdi, and still Tom seemed to be oblivious to all sounds and external stimuli. If Gaia hadn't known better, she might have thought her father had just gotten majorly stoned before dinner.

The hotel restaurant was equally as cozy as its rooms: small and intimate. Everything in this city seemed to be bathed in white flowing cloth and dark ornate oak. In New York everything seemed to be coated in a layer of grime—at least the spots where *she* used to hang out. The more time she spent here, the less the two cities seemed to have in common. And the restaurant had the perfect addition of candlelight and fresh purple and white irises at every table. Definitely a step up from Gray's Papaya or those fast-food dives on Eighth Street. Gaia felt oddly at home. But why not? Anywhere with her dad *was* home.

She took a sip of wine. It rolled on her tongue, filling her mouth with a delicious warmth.

Tom had insisted that, being in Paris, they *had* to drink red wine at least once. Gaia had balked at first. Frankly, even though she didn't mention this to her dad, red wine gave her the creeps. Not the *fearful* kind of creeps, obviously . . . just the feeling of being unclean. The reason was simple: Red wine reminded her of her "family dinners" with her uncle Oliver.

Man, to think that he'd actually *impressed* her with that—letting her drink wine with him. It made her stomach turn. She'd shared wine and delightful conversation with that demented freak, the man who'd actually killed her mother. How could she have been so blind to his lies and manipulations? It didn't just make her ill; it made her feel insulted, *enraged*.

But that was all in the past.

She smiled across the table at her father. It was so nice not even to have to speak. They could just sit here like this for hours. This was what being in a real family was all about. And now that Gaia looked back on it, those dinners with Uncle Oliver had felt like . . . *playing house*. It was as if Oliver were some sort of cardboard cutout of the perfect uncle. As if she'd wished for an uncle for Christmas, and Santa had just dropped one down the chimney for her, all tied up in an Armani suit. Like he was Streamlined Uncle Ken and she was Orphan Niece Barbie.

But now Gaia was in her own skin. She wasn't playing *anything* anymore. She even felt right in the one nice dress

141

she owned—the black one she'd bought with Mary and never worn. Finally. She'd known, maybe subconsciously, that it represented a part of her when she bought it, but it was a part that had been asleep for so many years, a part that had made her uncomfortable for so long, a part she could only have inherited from her mother.

She took another sip of wine. She had to admit, it felt good to give in. After all, her father hadn't suggested that they order a merlot to prove that he was some kind of "cool, permissive" authority figure. He was simply sharing something with his daughter. Something he liked. They were experiencing the elegant tastes of Paris *together*, as a family.

"Hey, Dad?" Gaia finally asked with a faint smirk. "Are you aware that you've had that same dopey smile on your face for the last five minutes?"

He laughed, then shook his head and shifted in his seat. "I'm sorry," he said, wiping his eyes cartoon style, as if he'd just awoken from a nice long sleep. "I think I've come down with some strange, exotic illness since we've been here. The symptoms are dopey smiles and unavoidable feelings of happiness."

Gaia glanced down at her wine, blushing slightly. "Well, I don't mind it so much," she mumbled. Incredible: There was a time—very, very recently— where even *that* small acknowledgment of emotion would have seemed impossible. But things were changing so fast. Besides, given all the time she'd yearned for his attention, it wasn't necessarily such a bad thing having him concentrate massive doses of it into such short sittings like this. No . . . it was like an I.V. of attention—like saline being pumped directly into the vein of a victim of dehydration. In a way, it was a necessity.

"So, Gaia?" Her father cleared his throat, and his expression grew more serious. "You're sure you're okay with me going out to meet my contact—"

"Yes," she insisted, giggling. This was about the tenth time he'd brought up the debriefing since lunch. The way he kept talking about it, apologizing for it, warning her about it . . . well, it was almost as if she were in the second grade again, and he felt guilty for not having arranged a baby-sitter. She knew he couldn't be around her every single second of every single day. He had a life. A job. An important job—one that demanded every bit of attention he could spare. And Gaia didn't want to interfere with it. Being in a family meant giving people space, too.

"I just hate to leave you alone," he muttered.

Gaia smiled. "You haven't left me alone yet."

"I know, I know. It's just that I can't stop worrying. It's foolish, but I can't stop remembering . . . you know, the last time I left you. Five years went by before . . ." He didn't finish.

Gaia's throat tightened. Her father never seemed

this unsure of himself, this awkward or inarticulate. Yet somehow it made him even more endearing. She felt a sudden urge to jump up from the table and squeeze him. If she didn't watch herself, she might burst into tears. She picked up the bottle and clumsily clinked the top to her glass, pouring a little more wine.

"I'm just gonna have a little more of this," she mumbled.

Her father forced a chuckle. "Good idea. Well, like I said, the meeting shouldn't take long. A couple of hours at most. Then I'm all yours."

"That's *fine,*" Gaia assured him. "Really." She took a sip of wine. "I can take care of myself, remember?"

He lifted his own glass. "I know. But you're just going to have to start getting used to the fact that someone *else* will be taking care of you, too." He flashed her a loving "so-there" smirk.

Gaia blushed again. This whole blushing thing was getting ridiculous. It must be the wine. Maybe she should lay off for a while.

"Look, Gaia," her father went on, switching again to a more serious tone. "There's something I want to tell you." He leaned down under the table and pulled a heavy manila envelope from his briefcase. It was old, battered—and several inches thick. "I keep waiting for the right time to give this to you. The truth is, I don't know if there will ever be a right time. Tonight is probably as good a time as any."

144

He handed the package to Gaia.

A flicker of electricity shot through Gaia's body as she took it. Whatever this thing was, it was heavy. She kept her gaze locked on her father's. He looked nervous. Scared, even. Shit. *Just don't let it be something bad,* she prayed, although her brain was a dull void. *I couldn't handle anything bad right now. Not now . . .*

"What is it?" Gaia forced herself to ask.

"They're letters," he said. He stared at the package with a cryptic, troubled expression that Gaia couldn't understand.

"Letters from . . . ?" she prompted him.

"From me," he replied.

"To . . . ?"

"To you."

Gaia's brow furrowed. She was beyond confused; she was totally baffled.

"I'm sorry," he said, taking the package from her hands and laying it on the table. "I just . . . thought you should have these. I guess I wanted you to read them." He paused uncomfortably again, avoiding eye contact. "They're all the letters I've written to you over the years and never sent. Well, not *all* of them. There are files and files of them all over the world, but this is the file I keep with me. And . . . I want to give it to you because, well . . . because I wrote them to *you*—every day when I could, sometimes twice. . . ."

Gaia looked down at the package and stared at it. She felt oddly detached, as if she were studying herself—waiting to see which of the thousand emotions running through her would manifest itself first. Would she cry from the sheer sadness of it all? The tragedy of all that time missed with her father? Or would she burst from the overwhelming love she felt for him at this moment, staring at the proof positive that he'd never forgotten her—as she'd believed for so long? That he'd actually thought of her every day, spoken to her even though she couldn't hear him? Or would she lash out at him? Slap his face for being such a fool and staying away from her?

That seemed to be what he was expecting, judging from the look of uncertainty on his face. But he didn't have to worry about that. Her anger had begun to fall away on the plane. Because in truth, at the very heart of it, Gaia hadn't spent the last five years pining for her father's *presence* or his *responsibility*. She'd known how to take care of herself since nursery school. What she'd yearned for all those years, and thought she'd lost, was his *love*. And here it was, sitting in a large manila envelope on the table.

Gaia couldn't stop herself anymore. She stood up from her chair, took two steps around the table, and hugged her father tightly.

"I'll read every one of them," she whispered.

"WHOA, THERE, ROLLING THUNDER!"

Inner Bitch

Ed threw on the brakes and looked up. The shrill voice belonged to Megan Stein. Wonderful. Just his luck. And she happened to be with Tina Lynch. In his attempt to flee school Ed had run right smack into the one group of people he was *not* ready for: the FOHs—Friends of Heather, as Gaia had dubbed them.

"Drive much?" Megan asked sarcastically. She shook her head, brushing off her long black skirt and white Agnes B T-shirt. "You know, being in a wheelchair doesn't give you the right to barrel around the halls at top speed."

Ed scowled. "No, it just gives us the right to get the best seats in movie theaters," he muttered.

Megan and Tina exchanged a confused glance.

"What are you talking about?" Tina asked.

Before Ed could think of an appropriately absurd reply, Heather rounded the corner. His head drooped. No . . . he definitely couldn't deal with the FOHs right now. Not in the wake of the news about Gaia's absence. Heather's friends didn't exactly allow Heather's finest qualities to shine. In fact, they seemed to go out of their way to nurture her inner bitch. Which was one of the reasons Ed was so relieved that she'd been spending less and less time with them—

147

"What's the matter, Ed?" Tina Lynch asked. "You look sad."

"Who, me?" Ed replied, pasting a smile on his face for Heather's sake.

Heather tried to smile back. But her eyes quickly darted to Tina and Megan. "Hey, guys," she said. "I was wondering where you were—"

"I've been meaning to ask you something, Ed," Megan interrupted. She didn't even acknowledge Heather's presence. Instead she put her hands on the back handles of Ed's chair, as if he were a human podium. Ed *hated* it when people grabbed the back of his chair. Especially people like Megan.

"What's that?" Ed grumbled.

"Well." She adopted a tone of exaggerated friendliness. "Maybe you can tell us why our friend Heather, here, has been acting like such a freak—"

"I'm right here, Meegs." Heather groaned. "You can talk to me."

And keep me out of it, Ed thought, clenching his teeth.

"What's the point?" Megan asked, glancing over at Tina. "Whenever we try to talk to you, you dis us. It's been going on for I don't even know how long. And it's got to stop." Her voice hardened. "So whatever your problem is, get over it."

"Word," Tina agreed.

Ed almost laughed. *Word?* Tina had been

148

listening to one too many rap albums recently. Whatever. Time to split. Clearly this little tiff had nothing to do with *him*—despite what Megan might think. This was between Heather and her friends. With a quick jerk he pulled himself free of Megan's grip and began rolling away.

"Where do you think you're going?" Megan called after him.

Ed glanced over his shoulder. "Somewhere else," he mumbled.

"Wait!" Heather shouted. "Don't just run off!"

He jerked the brakes, feeling anger well up inside him—then spun around. There was absolutely no reason why he *shouldn't* run off. "What do you want?" he snapped.

Heather's face fell. "I . . . I just—I don't know," she stammered, glancing at Tina and Megan again. "I just—"

"I think we should leave you two alone," Megan stated dramatically. She tossed her hair over her shoulder and nodded at Tina. The two of them thrust up their chins (which only made them look like lame third graders) and strolled down the hall—past Ed, vanishing into the mob of kids flooding toward the exit. It was just so . . . asinine.

He glanced back at Heather. She was shaking her head.

"Why don't you try to catch up with them?" he suggested.

She shot him an icy glare—as if he'd just suggested that she dive headfirst off the Chrysler Building. But then her expression softened. She stepped toward him. "I'm sorry," she murmured. "It's just . . . I don't know. I miss my friends. And I'm sorry I've been acting so weird."

Weird is an understatement. Ed swallowed. He lowered his eyes. At first he had been pleasantly surprised by this new, sensitive Heather. But now he wasn't so sure. Still, her apology counted for something, didn't it? At least she was aware of how strange she was acting. Which probably meant she wasn't going completely insane.

"It's okay," he mumbled. "You just have to stop worrying so much."

She nodded, sighing. "You're right. Let's talk about something else."

He glanced up and forced a smile. That was a good idea. And in fact, he did have some good news. "Well, I moved another toe last night—"

"You didn't tell anyone, did you?" she demanded.

Ed's eyes widened. The harshness of her tone shocked him. She hadn't even let him finish his sentence. *That's your only response? That's all you can think of?* He suddenly felt violently ill, as if he might vomit right in the middle of the hall.

"What?" she asked nervously, searching his eyes. "You did? You did tell someone, didn't you? You can't—"

"No," he barked. This was incredible. Freaking

incredible. Good news made Heather nothing but frightened. Pissed off, even. He looked into her anxious eyes. Somehow, with that skittish, self-obsessed look on her face, for the first time in all the time he'd known her, Heather looked . . . ugly. "I didn't tell anyone. The only person I told was *you*. I gotta go."

And with that, he clamped his hands down on his wheels and pumped them for all they were worth, whizzing down the hall and away from her as quickly as he could. He needed to be alone immediately—although he doubted he could possibly feel more alone than how he'd just felt with Heather.

"Wait, where are you going?" she called out.

"I have a lot of work," he called back, not even turning his head.

"Well, I'll call you tonight, okay?"

Her voice was lost in the noise of the hall. Good thing, too. Because Ed had no answer for her.

"ALL RIGHT, THAT'S IT! RISE AND

Happy Hour

shine, brother. Time to get up and at 'em!"

Sam heard a voice somewhere in the distance, but he was too groggy to know where it was coming from. Had he gotten drunk and joined the army or something?

"Who's there?" he mumbled.

The next thing he knew, the bright overhead light in his room tore into his eyes. *What the*— Two strong arms grappled his torso, yanking him into an upright position on his bed. Sam felt his body begin to fall back, but the arms kept him upright.

"Dad?" he muttered, trying to focus his vision.

There was laugher—wild, explosive laughter. The hands let him go. He heard footsteps in his room. What time was it, anyway?

"It's not your *dad*. It's Josh, you loser."

"Oh, hey, Josh," Sam croaked. His throat was dry. He blinked several times and squinted, finally focusing on Josh—who was bundled up in his gloves and overcoat, trying in vain to straighten out Sam's disaster area of a room.

"What are you doing?" Sam asked.

"Comin' to get you," Josh answered.

Sam shook his head, then toppled back down on the bed and pulled up the sheets. But Josh quickly ripped off the sheets and slapped his face a few times to wake him up.

"*Owww*," Sam slurred, annoyed. He sat up straight and rubbed his cheek. "What was that—"

"Come on, dude, enough with this depressed shit," Josh interrupted, fishing out a thick sweater and a pair of jeans from the flipped-over dresser drawer on the floor. "Put those on. We're getting out of this room *now*."

Jesus. Sam didn't want to know what would happen if he refused. Josh would probably slap him again. And truth be told, he was too groggy to argue. He simply did as Josh said and stepped dizzily into his jeans, throwing on a T-shirt from next to the bed and then the sweater. Josh lent a hand by throwing Sam's shoes at him—thwacking him right on the chest.

"All right!" Sam protested. "Christ." He laughed, feeling a little more coherent. "Are you trying to kill me?"

"I'm just trying to get you out of here," Josh explained.

"Why?" Sam asked. He bent over to tie his shoes. But Josh grabbed him off the bed and helped him on with his coat.

"Sam, my friend, it's five o'clock in the afternoon. And you know what that means, don't you?"

Sam shook his head—just as Josh grabbed a wool stocking cap off the floor and slapped it over him.

"It means that it's happy hour," Josh said. "It's time to get you happy."

For a second Sam just stared at the guy. A fleeting nausea tugged at his stomach. The last time he'd tried to "get happy" with booze, he'd wound up in bed with Ella—which, of course, was the first blind step into the huge, twisted pile of shit his life had now become. Part of him felt like telling Josh that he *couldn't* get happy. Happiness was an impossibility.

But another part desperately craved happiness. The thought of being happy filled him with longing; he almost felt like he was catching a whiff of some long-forgotten, delicious dessert he hadn't had since he was a kid. That was the part of him that didn't want to be alone . . . the part that feared Josh might vanish as quickly as he'd appeared, leaving Sam without a friend in the world. No, it was best not to question the one little bit of good luck he had. It was best just to accept Josh's offer.

ONCE AGAIN ED HAD FOUND HIMSELF

roaming the streets, trying to clear his head. After school he'd taken Houston all the way to the East River, where he knew it would be the coldest— hoping the freezing air would cool the boiling blood in his veins.

The Terrible Question

But no. Of course it hadn't.

So he'd turned around and headed home.

He'd been pumping the wheels on the chair so hard that his hands were beginning to cramp and blister. He couldn't even remember the last time that had happened. But that was no surprise. All his memories were foggy. So many new feelings and experiences were raining down on him that he felt like his brain had been dropped in a blender set on puree. For about forty-eight hours.

Well, he knew one thing for sure. There was no point in seeking solace at Gaia's house today—the way he had for so many months in the past. She wasn't there. She hadn't even *cared* enough to tell him she'd be gone for who knew how long. No, today Ed would just be going to his very own room. But it wouldn't be so bad. In his room no one could get to him, or disappoint him, or ask anything of him.

The apartment building offered sweet relief from the cold, and the elevator was even warmer. Ed hurried down the hall to his apartment, crammed his key into the lock, then rolled inside.

"I'm home," he called, slamming the door behind him.

No answer. Good sign. His parents were probably both still at work. He threw off his coat and moved straight for the kitchen. It was time for the world's largest milk shake, possibly two. Nothing else could possibly ease his pain—

"Little bro! What's up!"

But the pain was just beginning.

Victoria was there. Of course. He'd conveniently forgotten that she would be visiting while her new fiancé, Blane (he still couldn't get used to the sheer heinousness of that name), was on business in Milan.

Before Ed could duck and cover, Victoria threw her arms around him and planted a wet kiss on his cheek. Was it his imagination, or did her breath smell like she'd been drinking? It wasn't even six o'clock yet—

"What's up, stallion?" she cooed, rubbing the top of Ed's head.

He smiled—but at this particular moment, as his patience was at an all-time low, he realized something. If she didn't stop petting him like a dog in the next three seconds, he might have to slap her. As usual, she was overcompensating. The way she had at the engagement party. The way she had pretty much every single time she'd laid eyes on him since the accident.

The sad truth was that she could never truly accept a disabled brother. Not with her shallow value system and materialistic ways. From the day he'd returned from the hospital after the accident, all she'd done was avoid him—or else provide sickeningly sweet, ill-conceived pep talks about how he'd be "back on his feet in no time" . . . when she was only trying to convince herself.

Thankfully, she removed her hand.

"Hey, Victoria," he mumbled.

He'd forgotten how much he'd appreciate her avoiding him, in fact. She'd been so deeply offensive, condescending, and butt annoying, Ed had begun to do everything in his power to avoid her, too. But of all the days he would *not* want to see her, this one really had to take the cake. Especially considering the fact that this was the first time he'd seen her since his surgery. And oh, she was sure to go to town with that one—

"So!" she squealed, pulling a kitchen chair from the table and sitting on it backward, getting right up in Ed's face as she sucked down her mineral water. "Are you, like, so excited?"

So freaking fed up and annoyed, you mean! he screamed back silently.

For about the tenth time in twenty-four hours Ed felt nauseated. He couldn't even look at her—not with that disgusting wide-eyed thrill she clearly had at the prospect of having a "normal" brother again. Could she be any more transparent about it? Ed didn't think he'd be able to mask his contempt. Luckily Victoria was so deeply egocentric that she didn't even notice what was on Ed's face. She just assumed that whatever she was feeling must be what everyone else was feeling . . . or if not, then at least what they *should* be feeling.

"Hel-*lo?*" she went on. "I mean, this is like a miracle! It's, like, the best thing that's ever happened to you since that stupid accident, right?"

There was nothing stupid about my accident, Ed answered in his head. *How on earth did you get to be my sister?* But he still said nothing. Maybe she would think he'd gone mute and leave.

"I know, you're totally speechless, right?" She put her hand on Ed's knee. "God," she uttered, pouring on the melodramatic amazement, "you could just suddenly stand up and be, like, totally normal again. And you know what?" She lowered her voice to that bizarre gossip volume that only she and her friends seemed to indulge in. "I bet you could have Heather back like that." She snapped her fingers. "Like that."

Each blink of Ed's eyes was a countdown to his own combustion. It dawned on him that she could potentially keep talking for hours. He was going to have to get himself out of this.

"I mean, like *really* have her back, Ed, you know? Not just as a date to a party. Not just for show. How psyched would you be for that?"

Actually, that's a very good question. Kudos, Victoria. Kudos.

"Yeah," he finally said in a dark monotone. "I've gotta go now."

He tried to move around Victoria, but she wasn't budging. It was as if she'd been transformed into an android that went blank when other people were talking.

"Sooo . . . ? How soon?"

"How soon *what?*" Ed mumbled.

She laughed. "Come on, dummy. How soon till you're up on your feet?"

He couldn't believe this. Hadn't Mom and Dad told her *anything?* Well, they probably had, but she just didn't hear any of the parts she didn't like.

"I'm in physical therapy," he said, staring down at the kitchen floor for fear that he might try to strangle her if he met her gaze.

"Okay, okay. When's that done?"

"Done?" he snapped. "I don't know when it's done. It might never be done."

Victoria groaned in frustration. "Well, are you making any progress?"

Just the question he didn't want to hear. Just exactly the one and only question that could send him over the edge. The terrible question that made him see his sister's face and Heather's face as one and the same. He hated that. They *weren't* the same. But in this one instance, and this one instance only, the lie was better than the truth. At least the lie gave him a chance to tell his sister how he really felt.

"No!" Ed shouted, glaring up at her. "I haven't made a goddamn bit of progress! Can't feel a damn thing!"

Victoria's jaw dropped. "I'm . . . sorry," she whispered, her face frozen in shock.

"I know you are," Ed muttered. He started butting

his sister's chair bit by bit to get her out of his way. "That's the problem. You don't have to be sorry. This is my life. By the way, did you know there's a nice big fat chance that the surgery might be totally useless? I mean, I could just be good old crippled Ed for the rest of my life."

"Ed, no," she croaked, shaking her head. "Stop it. Things are going to change—"

"And what if they don't?" he interrupted. He kept ramming the chair. She hopped out of it, but he didn't stop. No. This was just the thing to let out some extra aggression. Yup. It was the kitchen version of a demolition derby. He pounded away at the chair—venting all his pent-up frustration, all his confusion, rage, and self-loathing for having to lie. . . . There was a sharp crack. The bottom doweling was coming apart. Good. The chair might make some nice kindling for a fire—

"Ed!"

Wonderful. His mother *was* home. She came running into the kitchen, just in time to witness his freak-out. It must have been something of a privilege to behold, given that Ed almost never behaved this way. He glanced up at Victoria, who had backed up against the refrigerator and was staring at him as if he were a rabid dog. He might have laughed if he wasn't so ashamed.

"What's happening?" his mother cried.

"Nothing, Mom," Ed mumbled, finally jerking to a stop. "I seem to have broken a kitchen chair what with this clumsy wheelchair." He felt like he was listening to someone else. *Uh-oh.* He really was losing it, wasn't he? `Time to beat a hasty retreat.` "Well, I better get on over to my room and start my physical therapy—because I know how important *that* is. I wouldn't want to let anybody down and *stay* in the chair."

Neither his mom nor Victoria made a sound. They just stared at him.

Ed spun out of the kitchen and raced into his room, slamming the door behind him and locking it. But then his mother came pounding on his door a few seconds later.

"Ed? What's wrong, honey—"

The phone began to ring.

At this point Ed just had to laugh. `Boy, shit really came in piles, didn't it?` That was Heather for sure. Ed ignored both the ringing and the pounding and pulled up to his computer to log on to his e-mail. Maybe Gaia had written—

No new messages.

Nope. She hadn't even e-mailed him. It was just another little dart piercing everyone's favorite new target—Ed's heart.

The phone kept ringing. His mother kept knocking.

"Listen, I'm sure Victoria didn't mean anything—"

161

"Go away, Mom." Ed pulled away from his desk, grabbed onto the handlebars above his bed, and hurled himself into bed.

Pain was becoming more and more meaningless to Ed every minute. Physical and emotional pain. He found himself numbing to all his sadness, confusion, and anger, too. Yup, it was official. Ed's heart had finally shut down from emotional overload.

Wouldn't Heather be just delighted to know . . . Ed couldn't feel a thing.

Katia.

   If only you could see our daughter. If only you could glimpse this lovely human being who carries around so much of you—who keeps you alive every day, with every breath she takes. If only you could see how she's blossomed in these five years.

   I've spent all this time feeling sorry for myself, but tonight, Katia, my heart aches for you, knowing you'll never have the chance to see how our daughter has grown, to see what she's become. The pride that has flooded my heart in these few days is for *both* of us, my darling. Please know that.

   She is truly a wonder, our Gaia.

   Observing her from a distance for so long, watching over her from afar, I'd never been able to perceive more than the merest fraction of the whole picture. The truth is, I've been in such awe of her strength and her flawless fighting ability—and perhaps most of all, her indomitable will to

survive, no matter what the challenge—that I never allowed myself
to see anything else.

But having spent these days with
her in Paris, with this rare chance
to talk to her, to listen to her,
unencumbered by Loki's presence—
I've come to realize that her mind
is the most wondrous part of all.

Yes, I taught her certain
skills. I've given her the tech-
nique and the fighting knowledge
and the sharp reflexes. But those
were just seeds. And now that the
trees have grown . . . well, it's
mind-boggling. With her gloriously
wry sense of humor and her gentle
compassionate soul, she's more of
an adult than half my colleagues.
And her beauty . . . this
refined, stunning mixture of
power and grace . . .

You see, all her most remarkable
qualities, I've discovered, are her
gifts from you. All *you*, Katia.

And now they are your gifts to
me. I thank you from the bottom
of my heart.

Sam was what-
ever one
called the
ideal
level of **sheer**
intoxication
cacophony
between shit
faced and
fall-down
drunk.

"THERE IS NO WAY YOU CAN HIT

that shot, my friend," Sam Moon hollered. He could barely make himself heard—or hear himself, what with the din of screaming college students and pounding beat of some rap-metal band.

Tequila Moonrise

"You will now be eating those words, Mr. Moon," Josh shouted back as he leaned over the pool table. That look on his face . . . he was like a panther ready to pounce.

Sam held his breath. His brain was swimming with drink and noise and just the sheer *fun* of the moment. Josh's eyes narrowed as he lined up an impossible bank shot with the nine ball. A hush fell over the crowd—the crowd being the flock of women that had formed around the table.

Not that Sam particularly noticed any of them. Crowds of college girls were par for the course at this place—The Naked Stump, an NYU hangout in a raucous black-box basement on Eighth Street. Sure, they were pretty. Some of them were stunning, even. But hey, they could all be single and willing supermodels, for all he cared. He was attached. He wouldn't make the same mistake twice. Never again . . .

Josh took a few practice motions with his pool cue. Then he let loose—*pow!* The cue ball exploded from the end of his stick and cracked against the nine ball, forcing it to ricochet into the opposite side pocket.

Sam just shook his head. He couldn't believe it. Josh had to be a hustler. Nobody was *this* good at pool.

"Driiiink!" Josh and the girls cried in thunderous unison, pointing their fingers in Sam's face and mocking him joyously.

A drunken smile appeared on Sam's face. *Another drink? Oh, boy.* Unfortunately, this had been going on for hours: Sam versus Josh in any number of drinking games. This game was something Josh called A Shot for a Shot. One man simply had to hit a shot set up by the ladies to make the other man drink. The only problem, of course, was that Josh was a *flawless* pool player. And the more Sam lost, the more drunk he got and the more *flawful* he became. *Wait a second. Is that a word?* Flawful? *Hmmm. Probably not.* Sam giggled. His vocabulary was getting worse, too.

Actually, there was one more problem: Josh had insisted they drink tequila for the entire evening. He said it was the only liquor that was guaranteed to obliterate Sam's depression and take his mind off his problems. Sam had agreed at the time (he'd been too tired, surprised, and out of it to protest)—the time then being five-thirty.

The time was now nine twenty-two, and Sam was whatever one called the ideal level of intoxication between shit faced and fall-down drunk.

Sam staggered over to Josh and patted him on the back. "This is a hustle, isn't it? Are you tryin' to hustle me?"

"Oh, you know I am," Josh replied in a wicked whisper.

Their self-appointed female fan club burst out laughing. Sam stared down another shot of tequila. He didn't even see who had put it into his hand. Whatever. Who cared? He ignored a mild lack-of-balance-meets-nausea and poured the burning liquid down his throat as fast as he could—bobbing his head back into an upright position and pumping his arms up triumphantly. He was met with a rush of loud, adoring applause. A waitress (who referred to herself as the Lime Lady) shoved a fresh section of lime into Sam's mouth.

Sam backed away from the Lime Lady and the pool table, swerving a little. He grabbed a pillar for support. The music seemed to swell. He couldn't make out any of the lyrics. It was all screaming, distorted guitars, over-amplified drums. But he didn't care. Sheer cacophony was what he needed. At this moment, this music was the sweetest thing he'd ever heard.

"Listen to this!" he shouted, pointing up at the ceiling. "This is my song, man! This song is about me!"

"What the hell are you talking about, dude?" Josh asked with a laugh. He grabbed Sam by the shoulders and jokingly tried to shake some sense into him.

"Who is this?" Sam asked. His voice was a little slurred. *Who izz-iss?*

Josh shrugged. "Some local band, I think." He

glanced over at the Lime Lady. "Hey, who is this band?" he shouted.

"They're called Fearless," the Lime Lady answered with a smile. "What do you think?"

"Iss-a greatess thing I ever heard," Sam answered, giving her a shaky thumbs-up. His eyes wandered over to the bar. A couple of kids from his dorm were there, staring at him with a look of what could only be described as contempt. Vicious contempt. Screw 'em. He was happy.

Step right up and see the real live smack-head murderer! It's free!

Yup, Sam's faith in humanity had seriously dwindled in the last few days. Had *anyone* ever heard of that little thing called innocent until proven guilty? What a joke. Everyone in this country was instantly guilty—unless you were incredibly rich or incredibly famous—and Sam Moon was most definitely neither.

But that's why this band was his new favorite band. He was just like them. He was fearless. Bring on the stares, the threats, the accusations! Bring them all on! He would survive! He would triumph—

"Hey, are you all right, man?" he heard Josh ask.

Sam turned to him. "Course I'm all right," he stated. He lifted his hand. "You know what, dude? I wanna make a toast."

Josh smirked. "Don't you need a drink to make a toast?"

"In a sec," Sam answered. He tried to stand as steadily as possible but ended up swaying in front of Josh's face. Oh, well. Better just spit it out. "Here's to you, man."

"Come on." Josh shook his head and waved off Sam's words.

"No, I'm totally serious," Sam insisted. "To you, Josh. I didn't even know I needed to get good and drunk tonight . . . and you were *there*. You were there. To good friends and mass obliterating quantities of booze!"

Josh smirked. "Uh-oh. You know what I think? I think you need to get outside and get some fresh air—"

"No, no," Sam interrupted. "I need to dance."

"Dance?"

Sam nodded vigorously. He felt like he was watching someone else as he broke into a wild jig, shaking his arms and hopping up and down.

Josh burst out laughing. So did the Lime Lady. Even the people at the bar grinned. Without a second thought Sam leaped onto the pool table. The girls around him gasped. But Sam was too blissfully smashed to care.

"Hey, everybody!" he shouted, as if he were about to start the world's drunkest and most sordid pep rally. "Guess what? Since I have *no idea* where the *hell* my girlfriend is . . . I'm starting a new dance in her honor!"

"What's it called?" Josh hollered.

"Well, thank you for asking, sir!" he called back. "It's called The Gaia. And it goes a little somethin' like *thee-us*."

With that, Sam exploded with an impromptu display of karate chops, sweeping roundhouse kicks, and the occasional disco hip swivel.

"Awesome!" Josh shouted, jumping up on the table and joining in.

Now people were starting to look away in embarrassment. But that didn't stop Sam. Oh, no. He and Josh came within inches of ripping each other's heads off with each kick. Sam couldn't stop laughing. Sweat poured down his face. The room spun around him. It was truly amazing: He had no idea who he was at this moment. He'd been transformed into some tequila-swilling butthead. But he definitely wasn't Sam Moon. And what a relief that was.

His mission had been accomplished.

Walking through Paris—especially at night—is like walking right into an impressionist painting. Specifically a Monet. (My dad taught me about art history, too.) There must be a hundred cafés along the Boulevard St. Germain, and each one has its own rich colors: slabs of dark forest green and velvety maroons, iron tables and Old World glass facades. And everything seems so much more colorful than reality. More vibrant. More romantic. You can almost feel the emotions of the people buzzing through the entire street.

But at the same time everything is strangely fuzzier when you get up close. That's really why it's like a Monet. You can't really zero in on anything—not a single condensation or glass clinking. The scene is clearest when you take it in at a distance. It's totally surreal in that same way. No wonder impressionism started in France.

And reading my father's letters was like that, too.

I couldn't really zero in on
one specific thought, one specific message he gave me. I could
only take in the whole thing. The
whole package. Five years of cor-
respondence. And to sit there, to
go back through time with him and
imagine all those moments when he
was thinking of me, talking to me
as if I were with him . . .

Well, to be honest, it was a
little too intense. He loved me
so much. More than I could have
hoped for. More than I would ever
let myself imagine. Sitting
folded up in my hands were all
the "I love yous" I'd missed all
these years. All the "I miss
yous" crammed together in one
envelope. But they were there.
They were all there.

And then it hit me: I'll never
get that time back. It's gone.
All that's left from the last
five years are these beautiful
letters and my horrible, crappy,

empty memories. All that time
without him. All that time to
practice hating and bitterness
and cynicism. All that time to
gorge myself on Krispy Kreme
doughnuts and wallow—

Oh, yeah. That reminds me. I
am never going to eat a Krispy
Kreme doughnut again. No, it's
not because I'm turning over some
lame new leaf because I'm so
happy. It's because I've discovered chocolate crepes. The French
serve them at pretty much every
single café, and one single crepe
contains about the same amount of
chocolate and sugar as an entire
box of Krispy Kreme doughnuts.

But back to the letters.
Actually, I lied: There is one
that I'm able to single out. It's
a perfect little pill to cure the
misery of the last five years.
And it isn't the most eloquent,
or the longest, or the most emotional. It doesn't have the most
"I love yous" or the most "I miss
yous." Actually my guess, from

the way it was scrawled in the corner of the paper, was that it was jotted down in about thirty seconds. But still, it's really the only one I need to read.

Hello again,
   Mission in Paris. So beautiful here. Someday I'll bring you here with me. I promise.
                    Love,
                    Dad

Something struck his head, and he went toppling to **losing the fight** the floor—right smack into the puddle of blood.

GAIA COULDN'T REMEMBER A

Sweet Betty Sue

moment when she'd ever been more exhausted. Of course there were her postcombat blackouts. After any fight her body would usually give out on her so completely that she felt like her heart had simply stopped pumping blood.

But this feeling wasn't like that. It wasn't a "dark" tired. It wasn't the unbearable drain that came with having to will herself to survive in spite of the odds ... or that gloomy, empty hamster-wheel feeling of going nowhere fast.

No, this was the kind of tired she hadn't felt since she was a kid. It was a birthday party kind of tired ... the kind of tired she would get after running and screaming for hours—stopping only for soda, cake, and candy. It was the sugar crash. The feeling of being finished. The feeling of absolute completion.

Of course, it was natural that she'd have a sugar crash, though. She'd eaten about nine crepes. Her stomach was bloated to the point of agony. And sitting at this dessert café wasn't doing much to ease her pain.

Where was everybody, anyway?

Gaia glanced down at her watch.

Three forty-five. Oh, man ...

She'd actually used only the streetlights to finish

her last letter. Her table was bare—bused clean without her even noticing. The café lights were turned out, a locked metal gate obscuring the beautiful windows. They'd probably reopen for breakfast in just a few hours. But right now the street was empty. Just a long row of dark stone buildings, black cobblestone, and lifeless cafés. Not a soul in sight. Not a sound but the wind bouncing off the buildings and down the endless street—

Footsteps. Gaia glanced around the corner. Two young men appeared. They paused when they saw her. Then they took a seat at her table. As if she'd been waiting for them. As if every other table were packed—and this wasn't the middle of the night.

They smiled at her. Gaia didn't smile back. She wasn't sure which smelled worse, the stench of liquor on their breath or the two-liter bottle's worth of cheap cologne they must have poured directly over their heads. Actually, worse than both of those odors was the smell of European testosterone, which practically floated off their bodies like steam from a piping teakettle. Funny: She remembered her mother warning her about certain French men when she was a little girl. But at the time she still didn't know what the word *lecherous* meant.

"*Bonjour,*" they said, with what they must have thought were their smoothest smiles. Gaia realized then that she was being unfair. Lechery wasn't strictly a problem of the French. She had seen plenty of guys like this before, roaming the streets of Greenwich Village after hours—accosting anything that looked remotely female, desperately trying to make up for another long night of rejection.

The one to her right wore a pink pin-striped shirt, opened at least four buttons to reveal as much of his black Brillo chest hair as possible. Not to mention the very thin gold chain that nestled itself somewhere in the forest of his neck hair. He had slicked back his black curls so that the top of his head was flat, but his hair flowed out in the back into a long frilly ponytail.

And the one on the left . . .

The collar on his lime green Lacoste shirt . . . was turned up.

That pretty much said it all.

"*Vous êtes française?*" the one with the ponytail asked her politely. *Are you French?*

It was a reasonable question. Any French girl in her right mind would have been safely tucked away at home by now—not sitting at a deserted café at four in the morning, dressed in black evening wear and stuffed silly with crepes. Gaia could play it either way. If she wanted to convince these boys that she was French, it wouldn't be a problem. Her accent was flawless. But the real test of their character was to see how they'd deal with her if she said she was American. What the hell? Why not have a little fun?

"You boys are gonna have to speak *English*," she bellowed in a thick midwestern accent. "I'm from Oklahoma."

Gaia thought the midwestern accent might increase her "innocent victim" status. It was a game she'd often played back in Washington Square Park. You had to lay the best bait to catch the biggest scumbags.

"Oklah-hooma?" the one on her right repeated.

He and his friend shared a complicit laugh.

"*Oui!*" Gaia laughed along, like a fool. Then she made a strained face, motioning with her hands in big circles as if she were trying to eke out the one or two French phrases she'd practiced before coming to France. "Uh . . . my name *is* . . . no, uh, in French now, okay . . . *Juh mah-pail* . . . Betty Sue!"

Gaia stuck out her hand in the Furry Ponytail's face to give him a nice strong Oklahoma handshake. He and his friend couldn't stop laughing. And the harder *they* laughed, the harder *she* laughed in response.

"*Bettee Soo*, uh?" He laughed mockingly, staring at his friend as he shook her hand. "*Philipe*," he said, pointing to himself.

Gaia flipped around and stuck out her hand to Collar Boy with a loud inquisitive gaze, waiting to hear his name.

"Thierry," he said, shaking her hand.

"Well, *helloo*, Phil and Tyrese!" Gaia shouted. "Como tallee-voo, I'm Betty Sue! Hey, that rhymes!"

All three of them began howling with laughter. But

amidst all the noise echoing off the empty street, the two men began to speak to each other in French.

"This one's going to be too easy," Philipe murmured as he continued to smile in Gaia's face.

"She's got to be the dumbest one yet," Thierry replied with a gracious grin. *"I can't wait to shut her big mouth."*

"Later," Philipe said. *"First I want to find out what her tongue tastes like."*

Bingo, Gaia thought. She should have known. A couple of lame, vile, idiotic victimizers. They were the same in any culture. Too bad their career was about to come to an abrupt end. She really missed this . . . this part of her past, the part devoted to cleaning the streets. She could barely contain her excitement, in fact. Her foot began to shake under the table impatiently. She had to wait for one of them to make a move. That was her style. But the anticipation was killing her. If one of them would just make a move, then she could finish her day with a full-force merciless ass kicking. . . .

"I had no idea you Frenchmen were all so happy!" she exclaimed.

"Ah, *oui*," Philipe agreed in his heavy accent. "*Very* happy."

They then discussed in vivid detail—in French, of course—how very happy they'd be to do certain things to Gaia—things that involved so many sickening and deeply offensive words that Gaia began to feel like she might not be able to hold on to her crepes. She might just have to start ripping them apart solely for their filthy minds. Yeah, screw physical provocation—

Philipe suddenly let out a singsong whistle that echoed down the deserted boulevard. Three more men emerged from an alley around the corner. An electric fizz hummed in Gaia's body. Interesting. There were five of them now. Five drunken vermin. Still no problem . . . just one that required a little more thought. Philipe casually motioned the newcomers over to the table—as if the street were simply one big party and his cronies had just happened to walk in. They all picked up on the comfortable laughter instantly, making social chatter in their native tongue as they formed a claustrophobic circle around her.

"Oh, *my*," she uttered.

SAM NEVER SAW THE GUY COMING.

He was too busy doing The Gaia with Josh. But it was actually kind of appropriate that the grand finale of The Gaia would involve getting sacked by some muscle-bound thug.

Basement Bloodbath

The thug had gone for the knees, taking Sam's support right out from under him. Sam went toppling off the pool table, hitting the ground with a hideous thud—but somehow not even feeling much pain. There was just enough awareness left in Sam's inebriated brain for reflexes to kick in: He threw out his arms to break his fall. His hands hit first, his head hit next (causing an explosion to echo endlessly through his seemingly hollow skull), and last came his shoulders and his knees—sending an agonizing jolt from each corner of his body that seemed to converge in the center of his back.

"Ugh," Sam groaned.

The thug rolled off him.

A moment after the initial shock, there was nothing. Sam's bones and head seemed to throb with a dull ache—but that was it. *Thank you, Mr. Cuervo,* he thought, smiling facedown on the reeking beer-stained floor.

But his happiness was short-lived. The next thing he knew, a pair of strong hands was lifting him off the ground.

Sam's mouth fell open.

It wasn't a thug at all. It was his former friend and former roommate, Brendan Moss. Actually, it was about three of them. And they were all very blurry.

"Brendan," Sam slurred, removing Brendan's hands from his shirt and straightening up as best he could. "What's up? Was that *you*—"

"You make me *sick*, Moon," Brendan spat at him. The furrowed brow and pinched-up nose said it all: He was disgusted. "Having the freakin' time of your life—it's disgusting. Are you on junk right now, you son of a bitch?"

"Brendan." Sam shook his head, trying not to laugh at the utter absurdity of the situation. This was insane. What were people saying about him, anyway? "You have *no idea* what you're talking about, man. It's *me*, for chrissake. *Sam*."

He reached for Brendan's shoulder, just to make some kind of familiar contact—but Brendan shook it off with a snap of his arm.

"Don't touch me, you psycho!" he shouted. He leaned in close, his face inches from Sam's own. *Blecch*. Sam grimaced. It smelled like Brendan had been drinking a fair share, too. "I don't know how you got Mike into that shit, but I hope you fry for it. Watching you laughing it up. Getting drunk off your ass when they just buried him a few *days* ago? *Dancing*, Sam? Like you're dancing on his freakin' *grave*, you sick shit—"

"All right, chill!" Josh shouted. He planted himself firmly between them, using his arms to drive them apart like a wedge. "That's enough!"

Brendan shoved Josh away from him. "Get off me! I don't even know you, man. For all I know, you're probably his *dealer*."

Josh laughed. "Actually, I'm his RA. And until

184

you've officially moved out, I'm yours, too, buddy."

"Brendan, please, come on," Sam said, making one last-ditch effort at settling this whole thing. But as Sam leaned forward, Brendan slapped his hand away violently. Sam gaped at him—and in that moment Brendan clamped his hand onto Sam's shoulder and rammed his tight-knuckled fist smack into Sam's jaw.

A white flash exploded in front of Sam's eyes. The force of the blow whipped his body into the jukebox, shutting the music down—instantly and completely.

"What the hell, man?" Sam barked.

"You want some more, Moon? Come on. Come and get it."

Sam rolled off the jukebox and rubbed his cheek. *That* hurt. He was beginning to feel a lot less drunk and a lot more pissed. Everybody was staring at the two of them, tense, silent. Did they want a fight? Fine. At this point Sam didn't care. He was ready to oblige. Brendan Moss was a moron. And luckily Sam saw only one of him now.

"Whatcha waitin' for, Moon?" Brendan taunted.

Nothing, Sam answered silently. *Nothing at all.* Rage poured through Sam as he charged, fueling both his aggression and attack. Sam faked with his left, but within inches of Brendan's face he threw a fast, hard right jab to dead center. *Dammit!* That hurt his knuckles. He'd actually felt something crack there, too—

Oh, shit.

Blood was pouring from Brendan's nose.

Brendan cupped his face and leaned over, howling as he watched the blood quickly puddle on the floor. Sam swallowed. He must have broken the kid's nose. He didn't want to do that.

"Brendan, man—"

There was a blur. And in spite of what he might have thought only an instant before, Sam *was* too drunk to fight. Something struck his head, and he went toppling to the floor—right smack into the puddle of blood. All at once he was being subjected to a barrage of wild punches, but he was too disoriented to fight back or even to see the next punch before it came. The assault felt like an avalanche of rocks and razor blades, cutting away at his face and his body ceaselessly. Not a moment of relief. Not a moment to breathe, just stinging pain after stinging pain, the frightened screams from the crowded bar, and Brendan's voice.

"Was I next?" Brendan growled as his fists rained down on Sam. "Was I next, you sick piece of—"

Brendan went flying backward off Sam. Just like that. As if someone had landed a hook in his back and reeled him away. Sam didn't think to question it. No, his only thought was to get out of there, as quickly as possible. He staggered off the floor and tried to catch his breath—wheezing desperately, propping himself up on the busted jukebox. But then he saw through his blood-obstructed vision that Josh had twisted both of Brendan's arms behind his back. It was *Josh* who had yanked Brendan away. It was Josh who had come to the rescue, once again. And now Josh was holding fast to Brendan, even as the guy tried to wriggle away.

"Come on, Sam," Josh grunted. "I'm sick of this asshole. Give him one good shot. Right in the gut."

But Sam shook his head. Attacking Brendan like that was something a coward would do. Something Brendan himself would do. No. He just stared at Brendan's bloodied face and channeled the remainder of his vengeful rage to his vocal cords.

"I'm not a killer! I did not kill Mike Suarez! I *didn't do it*, you get it? Is that clear enough for you?" Sam turned to the rest of the crowd, jerking his head wildly. "Does *everyone* get it? You're all a bunch of mindless *idiots* if you actually think I killed one of my best friends."

Brendan didn't say a word. Josh glanced at Sam, then shoved Brendan to the floor. Brendan landed at Sam's feet, falling into his own blood with a sickening smack. All at once Sam realized that people were screaming. And the screams were all turning into one loud, distorted buzz in his ears. The once flirtatious women had backed away, staring in absolute horror at the carnage.

Sam bit his lip.

Now that he thought about it, he was very queasy. He was very close to puking, in fact. . . .

Josh grabbed Sam's arm and squeezed it hard. "We gotta get out of here before the cops come, man!" he shouted. "Stay behind me!"

At this point the only thing clear to Sam was that Josh was in control of the situation. As usual. And Sam most definitely was not. As usual. So he simply shut off his mind and did as Josh told him. They elbowed their way to the club exit, cutting through the crowd and shoving any onlookers aside.

But it was too late.

Standing at the club exit were the cops.

And not just any cops.

Of course not, Sam thought. *Of course it would have to be them. If they weren't here, this wouldn't be my life.*

"MY FRIEND WOULD LIKE TO GEEVE

you a kiss," Thierry whispered in his thick French accent, leaning close to Gaia.

"Oh, I couldn't *possibly*," she drawled, holding a limp hand to her chest. Her thigh and calf muscles tensed—poised for a

One Last Chance

quick attack. But she kept her big, dumb smile plastered to her face as if nothing were wrong. As if she hadn't already heard what his friend *really* wanted to do to her.

"We would *all* like to geeve you a keess," one of the new guys said with a wicked smile. All the others giggled excitedly.

"Now, you boys better *stop*," she said, still pouring on the Betty Sue.

"Oh, come on, *bébé*," Thierry crooned, draping himself over her.

She brushed him aside and stood—very calmly, very quietly. If they wanted, they could still walk away. They could still save themselves. "Sorry, boys," she murmured. "I'm not that kind of girl."

"*Non*," Philipe growled. He bolted from his chair and grabbed her arms from behind.

Breaking free of his lame grip took only minimal effort. But as she spun around, she saw something she hadn't expected: a knife. The temperature of the fizz in her veins shot up several degrees. Well. This was exactly what she'd been waiting for, wasn't it?

"Thank you," she sang out.

"*Fermez la bouche, salope*," Philipe whispered. Translation: *Shut up, bitch.*

Gaia replied by cramming her elbow into Philipe's gut. His eyes bulged. As he doubled over,

189

she shot her leg out at his face with a lightning-swift side kick, sending him sailing back into the umbrella of one of the other tables. The back of his head struck the metal post with a clang, and he collapsed to the ground.

The other boys stared at him in shock. And fear.

"Do you want to end up like your friend?" Gaia asked them in French.

Thierry came running at her. Pitiful. She leisurely planned her counterattack as he lunged for her hips—swiftly grabbing him by his ridiculous upturned collar and slamming his head down on her knee. He let out a whimpering bark. It reminded her of a Chihuahua. He fell in a sniveling heap.

Two down, three to go, she thought. She maintained her defensive karate stance, waiting to see if another fool would be stupid enough to attack. They might be thinking that good old Betty Sue had just gotten a couple of lucky kicks in. For all she knew, the notion of a girl's beating the crap out of a bunch of guys might seem even *more* implausible to the French than it did to the sleaze back home.

Philipe had apparently recovered from her initial attack. And then he actually did something unexpected. Gaia realized how tired and out of it she must have been because she usually approached these situations like a game of chess . . . not only anticipating her opponent's next move, but his entire game plan, so that there could be no surprises. But Philipe cupped his hands around his mouth and hollered.

Three more men in hideous club attire came running from the alley.

They joined the others and formed a loose circle around her. The fizz was now at a fever pitch, but Gaia was perfectly calm. That made *eight* of them total. And unfortunately, as she had learned time and time again with a group of assholes: The bigger their mob, the less afraid they were to attack.

Like now.

Yup. They didn't waste any time. One of the new men, in a silk black running suit, obviously fancied himself a martial artist. He came at Gaia with a barrage of kicks he must have learned in some lame middle school competition. *Ooh. Scary.* When he finally reached Gaia, she simply tripped him and hurled the weight of his body into another guy—causing them both to topple over.

Two more men instantly followed, though. They came at her, frantically punching away. She flipped one of them hard onto his back, but the other made contact, getting a good uppercut on her chin that snapped back her neck. As pain surged through her body, she realized that the food and exhaustion and glasses of wine had slowed down her reflexes. To take on eight, she needed precision.

She didn't have it.

The one who'd made contact was huge, so she had

to take care of him first. She grabbed his wrist and twisted it in an inhuman direction. He cried in pain. She flipped his entire body on its back, sending his fat frame crashing against the concrete. But then there were two men holding her arms down—and then a hard punch to her stomach that hurt like a bitch, and another. It was all happening so fast; she couldn't focus. She used the support of the two men holding her to snap a flying kick at her assailant's face—then she jumped up and landed smack down on her captors' feet, causing them to cry out in agony and release her. That was the one advantage of fighting in evening wear: *heels*.

But before she could even regain her balance, they were at her again. There was another unexpected blow to her face, then a kick from behind. She found herself tumbling into another man's clutches. He flipped her around and choked her. They were like disgusting little growling savages, reveling in their collective violence. But she couldn't stop them. There were too many of them, moving in closer and closer—collapsing on Gaia, kicking and punching and shouting....

She wasn't afraid. She just knew she was in serious trouble. She knew that there was a chance she could die on this beautiful street. And that filled her with rage. She couldn't let her life go. Not now. Not when it had just turned itself around.

The Dark Smog

"SO WE GOT YOU ON DISTURBING the peace, assault, destruction of property. And I doubt very much you are of drinking age, Mr. Moon." Detective Bernard laughed. He couldn't have looked more ecstatic if he'd grown himself some actual hair. "Throw in the little matter of this *murder charge,* and *hooo-eee!* We've got ourselves a full-blown criminal here, Reilly!"

Reilly nodded. He looked about as happy as Sam had ever seen him, too. Terrific. They were having the time of their lives. Destroying *his.* Were all cops this sadistic?

"Do you just follow me everywhere I go?" Sam grumbled, still panting heavily from his bloody encounter. He and Josh were both pinned against the wall just outside the bar door—and the cops had conveniently positioned themselves to block the iron stairway back up to the street. There was no escape.

"Well, what do you know, Reilly," Bernard announced. "Mr. Moon seems to have *another* roommate's blood on his hands! Boy, this kid doesn't waste any time, huh?"

"Please," Sam moaned—practically begging at this point. "Just let me go home." He didn't even have the energy to be scared of the cops anymore. He didn't have the energy to be angry, or righteous, or speak up for himself. He certainly didn't have the energy for any more quasi-witty banter. He just wanted to go home and nurse his aching wounds and pass out.

"He didn't even throw the first punch," Josh muttered. "It was total self-defense, so unless you're gonna arrest us for a thirty-second bar fight, why don't you get out of the way so I can take my friend home?"

Bernard glanced at Reilly. They both shrugged.

"You know what?" Bernard said. "You're right. He should go home and rest up." With that, both he and Reilly stepped aside and made way for Sam and Josh to leave.

Weird. But whatever. Sam didn't want to waste any time questioning their newfound kindness. He'd never been able to figure out these two, anyway. He began to climb dizzily up the narrow iron staircase. It took a fair amount of focus and concentration at this point; the thing was like a fire escape. Each step sent shooting pain through Sam's limbs. Josh followed slowly behind, basically spotting Sam all the way.

"We want him nice and fresh for his indictment tomorrow," Bernard added.

Sam stopped in his tracks and looked back down at the detectives. "What?" he groaned, not sure he'd heard them correctly.

"Oh, did I forget to mention that?" Bernard asked with a sour smile. "I just found out today. The state deemed there was enough evidence. So Sammy's going to be indicted for the murder of Mike Suarez. Can you believe it?"

Sam knew that he should have felt terror at this moment—a whole new kind of terror. This was no longer a paranoid fantasy or an anxiety dream. It was no longer the thing he feared might happen. It was real now. It was happening. He knew that he should have felt more pain, more rage at the overwhelming injustice. . . . But he couldn't. He was maxed out. He was too exhausted to be anxious. Too saturated with tequila. His anger had been deposited into Brendan's head and gut.

Sam stared blankly into Bernard's eyes.

"I didn't do it," he said with robotic simplicity.

Bernard gave Sam and Josh his most smug smile yet.

"You know, that's just what OJ said. And no one believed him, either. See you at the indictment, Sammy."

Bernard and Reilly waved good-bye.

Josh looked down the stairwell and spat a disdainful gob of spit a few feet from the detectives. Then he turned around and helped Sam down the street.

"Come on, buddy," he whispered, with his hand on Sam's shoulder. "Forget them. Let's get you home."

Numbness. That's all there was: numbness. Josh supported Sam as they trudged down the next few blocks—step by step in silence, back toward the dorm. The only sound Sam made was the high-pitched wheeze of his stilted breathing, obstructed by the dried blood that had clotted his nasal passages and the corners of his mouth. Thoughts came in and out of his head. Yearning for Gaia. How would he tell his parents? What would he tell Mike's parents?

But no thought lasted for very long.

"Don't worry, man," Josh soothed. "We'll straighten this out."

For what must have been the hundredth time in the last few days, Sam wondered what he'd done to deserve a friend like Josh. The guy was like an angel—appearing out of nowhere when Sam needed help the most. *Divine* help. He was almost too good to be true, in a way. Here he was, an RA in Sam's dorm—somebody who was supposed to enforce the rules—and yet he had taken Sam out to drink, even though Sam was underage and it violated . . .

Wait a second.

An unformed thought scuttled at the edges of Sam's consciousness, like a bug in the shadows. But he ignored it. Paranoia had done enough damage. Josh was *good*. Josh was a *friend*. And suddenly it occurred to him: Josh deserved to know everything. He deserved to know the truth. After sticking his neck out for Sam for no good reason . . . yes. Sam needed to do this. Even if it meant risking the loss of Josh's trust. Josh needed to know the facts—before the police did.

Sam took a deep breath.

"Josh, I want to tell you something," he began tentatively, as they made their way up Fifth Avenue. "But it's going to sound kind of crazy. So the thing is . . . no matter how crazy it sounds . . . I need you to believe me. I mean . . . I just need you to trust me, Josh, I'm talking blind faith here."

Josh nodded. He didn't say a word. He just kept holding Sam up.

And before Sam knew it, everything was pouring from his mouth. The entire Ella Niven story. The seduction. The betrayal. The stalking. The night Sam had found the needle in Mike's arm and Ella had hinted that she was the culprit . . . and then the awful discovery that Ella was Gaia's foster mother— and, of course, that morning when he'd seen Ella's dead body in Washington Square Park. But in spite of reliving these horrors again, in spite of having to *articulate* them, Sam felt a strange relief. Everything had been pent up inside him for too long. He *had* to talk about it.

"Sounds pretty nuts, doesn't it?" Sam concluded.

Josh didn't hesitate for a moment with his response: "Not any more than anything else. I believe you. And I don't want you to worry, Sam. We're going to get you out of this mess, all right? We'll figure out something."

Sam nodded. But for some reason, when he should have been relieved (mildly, anyway) . . . a nasty inexplicable feeling began to rise up in his gut—a dreadful sort of sensation that polluted his thoughts like a dark, unexpected smog.

"There's something about this night," Sam heard himself say. "The way I just *nailed* Brendan . . . the way that *bar* was . . . this whole night feels . . . *evil.* Maybe that's too strong a word."

"Come on," Josh whispered. "You're just bugging out. You're under a lot of stress. A lot of stuff has happened to you. More than one person should have to go through, you know?"

"No, man," Sam insisted, trying to classify the sickness corroding his body. "I've just got this feeling about tonight. Like . . . the worst hasn't even happened yet, you know? Like something else just horrible is going to happen. Something . . . I don't know . . . the only word I can think of is *evil.*"

Josh just laughed—that same, easygoing laugh that had been music to Sam's ears from the start. "You're just drunk, my friend. Just drunk."

Napoleon of the Gang Rapists

THEY HAD GAIA'S ARMS PINNED to the cold concrete, the stark white light of the street lantern blinding her almost completely. She could barely see who would strike next or from which side. It was torture—like being locked in an interrogation room with some sadistic military commanders. A hard kick struck her ribs. Another pounded her thigh. Then they started dragging her along the ground, scraping the skin she'd been brave enough to expose in her dress.

Gaia didn't care about the pain, though. She didn't care about the bruises or the cuts or the scrapes. It was just the sheer frustration of losing that was killing her inside. Sure, it took *eight men* to subdue her. But that was no consolation. She'd lost—

No. Not yet. It's not over till I'm dead.

She still had her feet to work with, right? And she used them for all they were worth. When she glimpsed a pair of legs, she trapped them with her own like scissors, toppling one of the bastards to the ground. When she saw an available shin, she cracked her heel into it—as if there were a bull's-eye painted right in the center of it. She did every ounce of damage she could do. . . .

But the cold fact remained: There were simply too many of them. She'd always been able to take down three men easy. Four, even five with only a few bruises to show for it. But *eight?*

That was the sickest and most sinister part of this whole operation. The cold strategic planning of a gang rape. Gaia had never witnessed anything this sordid in New York City. And she'd certainly seen her fair share of scum. How many times had they pulled this off? How many women had been forced to suffer through this torture? The thought of it sent another surge of animal aggression through her legs as she kicked at anything within a four-foot radius, puncturing flesh, flipping any one of them that was off balance. But about four hands reached out at once, and after a few seconds' worth of struggle they managed to control her legs as well.

"Foutez-la sur la table!" Philipe commanded. *Throw her on the table!*

He was clearly the leader. The general. The Napoleon of the gang rapists. Gaia couldn't believe that this pink-shirt-wearing, frilly ponytailed ball of black fur could possibly be their leader. But then, of course, he *was* the most repulsive.

With two men securing each of her legs, they picked up Gaia's writhing body and slammed her back down on the iron café table. Thierry stood behind her head. He turned it up toward Philipe—making sure she could see him standing between her outstretched legs, grinning triumphantly.

"I swear to God, I'll crack every one of those goddamn teeth!" Gaia screamed, seething with a rage she'd never felt. It was the rage of a caged animal. The rage of somebody who had no way out. The rage of a girl . . . who was trapped.

"*Bouclez-la gueulle à cette salope!*" Philipe ordered. *Shut that bitch's mouth!*

Thierry slapped his hand over Gaia's mouth. She tried to bite it, but he was holding her head still with his other hand. That was it. Now she could only strike with her eyes. She glared at Philipe's hideous face.

"*Bloquez-la,*" he said. *Hold her down.*

If I could feel fear, Gaia thought, *this would be the time to feel it.*

Philipe slapped his hands down on Gaia's thighs and pulled her closer to him, pushing up her skirt. He reached down and unzipped his pants, and then he spoke to her in English.

"You are going to love thees," he promised with his repulsive grin.

Gaia felt no fear. But instead a desperate wave of sadness fell over her, bringing a rush of tears to her eyes. It was the sadness of knowing she would lose her virginity *here*. In this awful place. She wasn't going to share it with Sam. They'd decided to wait until she came back from her trip. To wait for that glorious moment. Now she regretted that decision with all her heart. That was all she could think about . . . all she could think about as she stared at Philipe's smile.

But then the smile suddenly vanished.

His head snapped down on the edge of the metal table as if a sledgehammer had just slammed it from behind.

And then rearing up in the shadows, Gaia saw a blur of a figure. The most wonderful blur she had ever seen.

Dad.

Before she could even process what was going on, her father had shoved his knee into the gut of another one of her captors, then slammed the base of his hand directly into another's nose. Blood gushed all over Gaia's dress. She hardly noticed. One of her legs was free. The mob was confused, disoriented. That was all she needed.

In a matter of seconds she unleashed a series of lightning swift kicks, ramming her heel into skull after skull. Three bodies toppled to the ground. Every ounce of rage she'd ever felt had been crammed into those kicks. Then, with a deft arch of her back, she sprang off the table and onto the ground, readying herself for battle. A smile spread across her face. Ah, yes. She was back in control. And nothing readied her for battle like the need for absolute vengeance.

Forget about quality. It was time to kick ass for *quantity.*

Every face, every body that was within her peripheral vision . . . they became nothing but moving targets. Gaia had transformed herself into a whirling dervish of various martial arts: kung fu, karate, jujitsu.

Two of the three she'd kicked to the ground approached. Gaia ducked under them both. She thrust her shoulders under their stomachs and flipped them onto their backs with a thud.

Another two came at her. She clamped her hands onto a table and kicked with both legs simultaneously, lashing out with her heels and striking each of their foreheads with pinpoint accuracy. They dropped to the ground.

She stood up in a combat stance. Her breath came fast. She was ready for more fighting, more vengeance . . . *more.* But there was no need. Her father was delivering a flawless roundhouse kick to Philipe's head. And Philipe was the only one left standing—the only one stupid enough to hang around. The few that weren't unconscious were already disappearing back into the alley, their footsteps fading into silence.

Philipe keeled over.

He didn't move. Nobody moved.

Gaia smiled. She was panting. It was strange, though. Even though she and her father had won, Gaia could still feel Thierry's hand over her mouth—a phantom of the crime she'd almost suffered. . . .

The distinct two-note sound of a European siren began to ring in the distance. Someone must have finally called the cops. Her dad, no doubt.

Gaia stepped over to Thierry. His inhuman face was smeared with blood. His breath came in short gasps. She straddled him and clamped her hand over his mouth. His eyes widened in terror.

"Do you know what it feels like to be held down like that?" she whispered. *"Tu sauras en prison." You'll find out in jail. "Tu sauras—"*

"Gaia?" her father called.

She turned to answer him—but at that moment the shadows on the boulevard seemed to rise up and tackle her down into a sweet, black sleep.

Can someone give me one good reason to get out of this bed? I can't think of one. No point in doing my physical therapy. Who am I supposed to walk for? Brian, the wrestling physical therapist? Brian will be just fine whether I walk or not. Am I supposed to walk for Heather? Heather doesn't want me to walk. Am I supposed to walk for Gaia? Gaia doesn't care. For all Gaia knows, I could be rolling around in some Mexican whorehouse.

Am I supposed to walk for my family? Not as long as my sister is a member.

Am I supposed to walk for *me*?

I don't even know anymore.

You know what I wish? I wish I'd never had the surgery in the first place, that's what I wish. All this time I've been dreaming about going back in time. But I went back too far. I don't want to go back a few years. I just want to go back a few months. Back to when a good time was a

couple of solid eleven P.M. milk-
shakes and a phone conversation
with Gaia. That's what I miss
the most. Gaia.

Can you believe that? I miss
Gaia more than walking.

But there's no point in going
to school. She's not there. And
Heather is. And I don't want to
talk to Heather.

So, to sum up.

I don't want the distant past.
I can't have the recent past. I
hate the present. And I'm dread-
ing the future.

Who wouldn't want to be me
right now?

His emotions
were still
floating
somewhere
delicious
underneath
the **warmth**
river of
alcohol in
his veins.

SAM TRIED TO KEEP HIS ROOM

from spinning, but it was no use. The entire dorm seemed to be tilted on a forty-five-degree angle, rotating around him at a slow and even speed. He sat hunched over on his desk chair in the center of the floor. He was

Sign In, Sign Out

quite sure that he was sitting in silence, but a loud buzzing drone pulsed in his ears like the rumbling hum of a power plant.

The taste of blood and tequila was a foul mixture, but Sam had still been uninspired to wash the blood from his face or to rinse out his mouth. He hadn't even changed his filthy clothes . . . or looked over his wounds.

He wasn't motivated to do much of anything. His emotions were still floating somewhere underneath the river of alcohol in his veins. So he sat there. Thinking numbly of the nature of life in prison, with nothing to look at but dank gray walls. Nothing to do but sit in an eight-by-eight cell and yearn for Gaia, wondering what she was doing, whom she was with out there in the free world, envying whomever that might be madly—

Josh came barging into his room.

Sam barely looked up.

"Oh, man," Josh groaned with a mocking giggle.

"Have you just been sitting in that chair since I left you?"

Josh seemed to be speaking and moving at such a higher speed than normal, like a turntable's spinning too fast. Every reaction of Sam's came at a two-second delay.

"Yes . . . ?" Sam finally replied, not sure he'd even remembered what the question was.

"Well, I've got something to change your mood, my friend," Josh whispered. He was panting. He snapped a piece of paper right in front of Sam's nose.

"That's good," Sam said in a dull monotone, unable to focus on anything.

"Didn't I tell you I'd take care of everything?" Josh asked, slapping Sam's bruised shoulder, almost knocking him off his chair.

"Hey!" Sam barked. *That* was enough to get some feeling going inside him . . . but then that faded, too. It was only pain. Only physical. Only fleeting.

"Sorry, sorry," Josh mumbled with an impatient laugh, still flapping the paper in front of Sam's face. "Just *check it out!*"

Finally Sam's eyes zeroed in on the page.

Then he stopped breathing. He instantly saw it for what it was: a slightly forged sign-in sheet from the chemistry lab, dated the night that Mike was killed. And there was a nice empty slot placed in the center of the list. Josh didn't need to explain a thing to him. The paper said it all. Somehow Josh had gotten hold of this . . . and all Sam had to do was sign in his name. Sign himself out for the end of the night.

"It's so simple," Josh whispered, "but it's the *perfect alibi.*"

For a moment Sam couldn't speak. His mouth was very dry. The implications of this . . . well, he didn't even want to consider them.

"Bu-But I already told those cops I was at a movie," he croaked. He felt like he was listening to somebody else. "I told them I was at the Angelika—"

"No big deal. You just went to the movie *after* the chem lab. The problem is *solved.*" Josh slapped the sign-in sheet down on a book from the floor, placing it on Sam's lap. Then he pulled a pen out of his pocket and thrust it into Sam's hand. "All you have to do is *sign*, dude."

Sam's wits were barely functioning. He didn't even know if this was *real.* In the depths of his hangover everything had a terrible, hallucinatory quality. Why create a lie when in truth he was innocent?

Then again, who was going to buy the truth of his innocence? All indications thus far seemed to answer that question. *Absolutely no one.* No one except Josh. And even Josh seemed to think that he needed a lie to get out of this. But still, he wasn't placing the pen on the paper. With his emotions shot and his reason out the window, he could only act on some distant instinct in his cloudy brain. And again he felt that dread uncertainty, that same fleeting sensation he'd experienced earlier tonight . . . if Josh was supposed to be an RA, then why was he encouraging Sam to break the rules?

"Sam," Josh said. All at once his tone was far more serious and concerned. "Who's gotten you through this thing so far?"

Sam stared down at the paper. "You have," he whispered.

"So let me get you all the way out of it," Josh murmured. "I don't think you've got a whole lot of other choices right now, man."

That was all it took: the voice of reason. The voice that uttered the truth. He had no choice. He had to sign in to sign out . . . out of jail, out of agony, out of the terrifying mess his life had become. With a trembling hand (he didn't know if that was from trepidation or booze), he picked up the pen and signed his name. Twice. Both in and out of the chem lab, next to the time slots Josh had left open for him. Then he handed Josh the paper.

Miraculously, his hand stopped shaking.

"Thank you, man," Sam said as Josh stood up above him.

"No sweat, Sam," Josh replied.

"I owe you one," Sam said. "Again."

Josh smiled, folding the paper into a neat square. "I know, dude. But that's cool. I mean, I know you'd help me out. I mean, if I ever needed a favor from you . . . you'd help me out, right?"

"Of course I would," Sam replied, without a moment's hesitation. But for some reason, that odd sensation was stronger than ever.

GAIA AWOKE TO FIND HERSELF LEANING

against the window in the backseat of a car. When she looked to her right, she saw her father, staring out the opposite window as a blur of French architecture flew by outside.

Homeward Bound

"Hi," she said sleepily.

Her father's eyes lit up. "Welcome back," he said, squeezing her hand.

"*Ow.*"

"Oh. Sorry. Are you all right?"

Gaia considered any number of witty retorts she could make to prove her nonchalance and her maturity . . . but none of them seemed appropriate right now. Her body ached too much. Her mind was swimming with terrible memories and wondrous relief. So the most mature response was the simplest.

"I'm alive," she said. "And I'm with you."

He nodded.

"How did you find me?" she asked.

"I saw that you weren't in bed, so I asked the concierge. He told me Boulevard St. Germain." A tired smile crossed his face. "Obviously I *can't* leave you alone for a few hours."

Gaia laughed. "Guess not."

"But it looks like I won't have to again," her father said.

"What do you mean?"

Tom flashed her a grin. "The meeting with that contact . . . Loki's been secured. No technicalities. No escapes. It's official. We can go home."

Gaia blinked, not comprehending. "You mean New York?"

"New York," Tom confirmed.

"You and me?" A delicious warmth shot through her body. "To live?"

"To *live*," he echoed. "I had them pack your things at the hotel. We're on our way to the airport now."

She smiled. She and her dad. Back in New York. With Sam. With Ed.

It was . . . perfect. It simply had no flaws in it whatsoever. It was Gaia's ideal existence. Yes, she'd thought she wanted to live in Paris for the rest of her life, but her last experience had forced a rather large shift in her perception of the city. Idealize anything too much and you're bound to be disappointed at some point. Not that she wouldn't always love Paris, but she could certainly stand to be away from it for a long while. And what better place to be than her other favorite city, with her father, and her lover, and her true friend?

It was her first chance since her mother's death for an actual life. A delightfully simple and unremarkable life. A home.

Gaia gave her father a nod. "I have no problem with that," she said.

THE PRISON GUARD SLID HIS HEAD

His Own Psychiatrist

slowly from left to right, ensuring that no other guards or inmates were in sight. He turned at just the angle so that his back obscured the view of the surveillance camera at the end of the long gray hall, and then he slipped Loki a note through the minuscule slot below the window of the solid steel door.

To: L
From: BFF
Date: February 5
File: 776244
Subject: Gaia Moore
Location: Boulevard St. Germain

Subject attacked at 4:17 a.m., Paris time. Nearly
raped. Eight assailants. Enigma provided combat
assistance and rescue. Subject and Enigma worked in
tandem to defeat assailants. Eight in police custody.
Subject smiled, embraced Enigma, and collapsed.
Enigma carried subject to black sedan and departed.

Awaiting further instructions. Please advise.

Loki crumpled the note furiously and dropped it
to the floor, staring out the small window of his enor-
mous cell door at that same damn dank gray wall that
he'd been staring at for days. His head ached as he
imagined Tom and Gaia fighting off a group of thugs
in tandem like some damn comic book or cartoon. *A
dynamic duo.* How very heroic. How very sickening.

*I am the one Gaia should be embracing. Not him.
Gaia belongs to me.*

Tom might have taken Katia from him, but the
chances of his taking Gaia as well were absolutely nil.
Loki would see them all dead before he let that happen.

215

I'll destroy you, Tom, he swore to himself, pressing his hands to the door.

He knew what was happening. Oh, yes. He could analyze his own emotions as if he were his own psychiatrist. The frustration of being locked in purgatory had finally begun to cut through his numb protective shell.

But my vengeance will be pure, brother. I will not make the same mistake twice.

Loki dropped to the floor of his cell and picked up the crumpled memo. He pounded viciously against the door twice, pouring all his frustration into his cold fist.

A pen slipped through the slot.

Grabbing the pen, Loki smoothed out the memo against the door and scrawled his response furiously on the wrinkled paper, dispensing with the formalities. Then he crumpled it again into a minuscule ball and slammed his hand against the door once more, slipping the note and the pen back through the slot.

MEMO: Not another word about their smiles or embraces or you will be terminated. Just confirm that the New York plan is still moving along smoothly.

They're real, and they're here...

When Jack Dwyer's best friend
Artie is murdered, he is devastated.
But his world is turned upside down
when Artie emerges from the ghostlands
to bring him a warning.

With his dead friend's guidance,
Jack learns of the Prowlers. They
move from city to city, preying on
humans until they are close to being
exposed, then they move on.

Jack wants revenge. But even as he
hunts the Prowlers, he marks himself—
and all of his loved ones—as prey.

Don't miss the exciting new series from

BESTSELLING AUTHOR CHRISTOPHER GOLDEN!

PROWLERS

POCKET PULSE

PUBLISHED BY POCKET BOOKS

3033